P9-BYO-575

HOWARD'S BAG

Fiction by Douglass Wallop

Howard's Bag
Stone
The Good Life
The Mermaid in the Swimming Pool
So This Is What Happened to Charlie Moe
Ocean Front
What Has Four Wheels and Flies?
The Sunken Garden
The Year the Yankees Lost the Pennant
Night Light

Nonfiction

Baseball: An Informal History

∗ HOWARD'S BAG

a Novel by

Douglass Wallop

W · W · NORTON & COMPANY · INC ·
NEW YORK

Copyright © 1973 by Douglass Wallop

Library of Congress Cataloging in Publication Data

Wallop, Douglas, 1920–
    Howard's bag, a novel.

    I. Title.
PZ4.W215Ho [PS3573.A44]   813'.5'4   72-11777
ISBN 0-393-08674-7

ALL RIGHTS RESERVED

Published simultaneously in Canada
by George J. McLeod Limited, Toronto

PRINTED IN THE UNITED STATES OF AMERICA

2 3 4 5 6 7 8 9 0

HOWARD'S BAG

✳ one

One summer in the state of Connecticut, a middle-aged burgher developed a late-blooming interest in truth and honesty.
Until then he had been a consummate liar.

It was during the time of President N., and a blight lay
heavy upon the land, with little joy anywhere, not in the
daily press, not in the stock market, not in the hearts of men.

The burgher was Howard Carew, a certain homeowner in
the incorporated township of Welton, where he had lived
for years and years, threading his way through life as best he
could, lying his head off.

Howard Carew was a liar in word, in deed, even in
thought. Lies, he had convinced himself, were the oils and
unguents of life, at all levels of existence, particularly at the
domestic level. Lies were a form of courtesy, of chivalry, even
of compassion. Blunt, coarse tellers of truth, so loud, so full
of self-regard and braggadocio, had always been repellent in
his eyes. Such creatures he found destructive, using the truth
as a club which they wielded with cruelty and arrogance and
even low vengeance. Hardly less reprehensible were those
truth-tellers who spoke with a low, intense sincerity and a
show of love for their victims. About these there was a certain
ethereal sibilance that Howard found most unattractive. He
preferred lying.

Having been so long a liar, Howard lied with grace and
artistry and with total good cheer. The trick, in his mind, was

7

to play it always low-key. If possible one should never lie in a sweaty, excited way. Lies told in a loud voice, with a big business of looking someone, his wife or whomever, straight in the eye—these lies were clumsy and suspect. Far better was the guttural lie, told casually, monosyllabically, sometimes with a yawn or a sigh, all with an abstracted air, as if the mind actually were on something else. A faraway look often helped lend an air of truth.

Midsummer found Howard well along in a sporadic liaison he was conducting with one Sadie Fitch, a frequently unemployed actress who had come to New York to seek her fortune—and found Howard. Sadie had no idea what a huge liar he was. Neither did his wife, nor the members of his community, nor his associates at the office. For a man to be *known* as a liar, of course, says very little for his skill at lying, and Howard was very very skillful.

So entrenched was he in his way of life, and so smoothly were things going that Howard had no conception of what lay ahead. The first hint of possible change came on a humid day in early August.

The day started quite normally—that morning Howard was lying with characteristic deftness and to apparent good effect. The previous evening he had spent *l'heure bleu* and then some at Sadie's apartment in Manhattan. Howard at breakfast next morning in Connecticut shook his head, stared into the middle-distance, and said, "I don't really understand that old bastard Lorimer."

It was barely seven in the morning and Charlotte Carew, his wife of more than twenty years, was still groggy with sleep, something Howard counted upon, because he had found that one of the best of all times for lying to a wife was when the wife was groggy with sleep. Charlotte wore a light blue robe; her eyes were blue and dreamy, her hair flaxen and straggling. Turning from the sink, she sat down and sipped her coffee. She cleared her throat, cleared it again, and asked, "Why do you say that?"

It was the question Howard had been waiting for. He was all set. "Oh, I don't know." He shrugged. "He just irritates me, damn it. Last night—oh, hell, it's not even worth going into."

"What happened?" Charlotte seemed only mildly interested.

"Well—it's waiters, I suppose," Howard said, letting his voice fade.

"Waiters?"

"Yeah, he's such a son of a bitch with waiters. He embarrasses me."

"You mean you had dinner with Malcolm Lorimer? Again —last night?"

It was the moment of the outright lie, and Howard met the moment as he had planned—with a forlorn nod and a faraway look. He was staring head-on at a can of salted peanuts which stood on the kitchen countertop, as if to give the impression that he was staring right on through the peanuts, directly at the imaginary scene in the restaurant with the imaginary waiter and his boss, Malcolm Lorimer, with whom he had not dined in months.

"What happened?" Charlotte asked. "What did he do?"

Howard took confidence from the sleepy, casual way she put the question. He shrugged again—shrugs were very good. "It's not so much what he did. It was his attitude."

"What?" Charlotte was at the stove, rattling the coffee pot. "I couldn't hear you."

"I say, it's his attitude. People don't go around nowadays treating waiters like an inferior brand of humanity. I couldn't stand to watch it." Howard sighed and shook his head.

9

Charlotte sat down again with her refilled cup. In spite of the coffee, she still seemed properly groggy. "Of all people," she said, yawning.

Howard shrugged again—his third shrug in a matter of minutes. "Well . . . hell . . . what difference does it make? I don't know why I should give a damn. What are you planning to do today?"

"Me?" Charlotte yawned. "Paint, I guess."

Over the years, partly for want of children, Charlotte had been painting and painting, and she had gotten steadily better. In Howard's wallet was a newspaper clipping which he carried with pride. It said:

THE
MARZOLF
GALLERY

Presents

Charlotte Spencer, American

First showing in New York—
Sensitive interpretation of
Nature in oil on large canvases

The showing had taken place that spring, and an influential art critic had written that her work showed a "flow and ebullience" and that it was moreover a "yea-saying affirmation" of nature.

Howard now found himself mildly puzzled about the way she had said, "Paint, I guess." From the look in her vague blue eyes, she seemed discontented or disturbed about something, and this struck him as unusual. Not that she was altogether lacking in discontent, but she didn't normally show it in the early morning hours when she was still so groggy that she could barely make it to the stove and back. She looked up from her coffee and shrugged. "Paint and read. What else?"

"Well, what's wrong with *that?*" Howard demanded. He

gave her a reassuring smile. "That's not too bad a life, it seems to me."

Without thinking, he carried his dishes to the sink.

"What are you doing that for?" she asked.

"Doing what?"

"The dishes. I'll take care of them."

Back in the early years of marriage, Howard had a good friend named Charlie Voigt, who once had told him: "Show me a man who helps with the dishes and I'll show you a man who's committing adultery."

It was a remark Howard had never forgotten. For years and years he had been careful not to help with the dishes. He wondered what had made him carry his dishes to the sink just now and absent-mindedly begin running hot water over his egg yolk.

In a surprisingly alert tone, considering the hour, Charlotte said, "All those dinners that you have with Malcolm Lorimer —who pays?"

"He does. Of course." Howard turned off the faucet.

"Always?" Her voice now was positively vibrant. It had a ring to it.

"Sure." Howard felt strongly that it was high time to get the hell out. Quickly he was at her side, brushing her hair with his lips. "Bye."

"Will you be home to dinner?"

"Absolutely."

"Good." Charlotte rose from her chair. "Do you have your Rolaids, sweetie? You look sort of jowl-y this morning."

Deep in a forest, high on a hill, thirty minutes from the railway commuter line—here was Howard's home, embowered and embedded in the Westport back-country, reached by a network of roads highly confusing to the casual motorist.

Careening down the long slope to meet the 7:56, and then

boarding the train, badly hung over, acid of stomach, weary of limb, Howard found himself disturbed by Charlotte's reaction to his story about Lorimer. Suave and expert as he was at lying, he was not accustomed to having his lies challenged, not even by the slightest nuance. Like any liar, however, he was on the constant lookout for nuances—and he felt he had detected a few. Perhaps he had overdone the part about the waiters. In fact, maybe he was overdoing Lorimer. Taking a quick count, he realized that he had used dinner-with-Lorimer as his cover-story at least four or five times in the past month. It was true that his cover stories tended to run in streaks. He got crushes. Finding a rich vein, he mined it for all it was worth. In June and early July, for example, one might have thought he had developed an incurable passion for attending night baseball games at Yankee Stadium. Instead of running in streaks, perhaps he should try for greater variety and balance. He would get a little rest and relaxation on the train and think it over but it seemed clear that for the time being at least he had squeezed all the mileage possible out of Malcolm Lorimer. He would give his brain a rest and then tackle the problem head-on. He closed his eyes.

To some men who worked in Manhattan, the commuter ride was a necessary evil, the price they paid for the stated privilege of housing their families in the far-off glades and dells. On the long morning and evening journeys, some whiled away the time with a thorough reading of the *New York Times* or other reading matter; some played bridge, some chess, some used the time to get paper work done. For Howard, however, the ride was a time of recuperation, of dozing, of drifting and dreaming—and often for plotting and scheming. With the steady deterioration in service, the rides were averaging nearly two hours in each direction and whatever other encroachments might be made against his time, he could always be certain that these hours were his private wealth. He prized them. They offered the relaxation that was so necessary for the conduct of what had become a highly complex life.

Howard had not always been a philanderer, nor for that matter such a monstrous liar. Back in the early days of marriage there had been a few episodes, none serious, one-night stands here and there, often bumbling, certainly nothing to scorch the pages of memory. In those days he had still clung to a sort of grudging idealism. But this was in the days before he moved out to Connecticut, before he began journeying in the company of other men to his place of business each day on the commuter train. Very soon he began to feel envy of these other men, even resentment. Whatever the facts may have been, they, in his mind, were a bunch of accomplished Don Juans, living sneaky lives, philandering in Manhattan, wearing inscrutable husband-masks in Connecticut, and resting up between-times on the train. Everything he heard and read led him to believe that for his fellow commuters life was a lip-smacking *rondelet* of infidelity.

For a while longer he resisted. He joined a bowling league, he pursued a passionate love of tennis, learned how to tie trout flies, bought a saber saw which enabled him to cut arcs and circles, built Charlotte a studio off the kitchen, took up horse-shoe pitching, gardened. These pursuits were pleasant enough in themselves but in the end they did not measure up.

Back in the days when he bothered to puzzle over such things, Howard had wondered about his need for the likes of Sadie and her predecessors. He knew it was not mere lust, knew it was something beyond polygamy or philogyny. Modern man's life being what it was, he had concluded that much of his need might be a simple yearning for derring-do. To set up a rendezvous with furtive phone calls, to slink into an apartment or hotel or motel and, some hours later, to slink out again; to return home on the 10:57, simulating the honest fatigue of a man who had done an honest day's labor; to invent outlandish excuses and cover-stories—taken altogether it added up to the elaborate machinery of high adventure, of a sort available to men of moderate means and modest physical stamina, men neither wealthy nor hardy enough to assail the Himalayas, nor damn-fool enough to sail a thirteen-foot boat around the world.

For all his aberrant behavior, Howard was in many respects highly conservative. At the time, current in the land was a male fashion trend toward floppiness and peacock coloration. It was a trend Howard despised. On his lap, covering an as yet unread *New York Times*, was a neatly folded grey jacket with a fine, barely discernible pin stripe. His button-down shirt was a pristine white, his black figured tie was resolutely narrow, its knot defiantly small. His once black, now greying, hair, abetted by a hairpiece, was full on top and rather heavy at the temples, a version of what his barber was pleased to describe as the "Rhett Butler cut"; and although it was not a description Howard would have used in speaking of his haircut to others, it was nonetheless a description which gave him pleasure.

In an age of hirsute embellishment, Howard was cleanshaven. His face was heavily sun-tanned, mostly from tennis, and although it was now in respose and showed a certain placidity, anyone watching him might have decided from the movement of his lips and his frequent swallowing that his stomach was bothering him. It very often was. There had been many mornings such as this—mornings after unwisely subjecting his digestive tract to the martinis and richly seasoned food that so often seemed to be the lot of the practiced philanderer, whether taken at a restaurant or taken at the hands of a cook such as Sadie, who cooked carelessly when she cooked at all. It was hardly surprising that Rolaids to Howard were indispensable equipment, his *sine qua non,* and as the train dawdled out of Darien, he reached into his shirt pocket, peeled loose his third and fourth Rolaids of the morning and popped them into his mouth, all without ever opening his eyes.

A penetrating observer might have noted something else about his face. Although it was lined and seamed with creases, and although it had the craggy look that often is confused with strong character, it was not a strong face. It showed the anxiety that might be expected in the face of a man whose two main goals in life had become to (1) do what he pleased and (2) keep his wife from finding out about it. Even if there should come a day, or night, when she found him in bed with somebody he would set up a stout denial. He would say, "You're wrong, it's not me, I'm not here, no kidding." And he would say it with a straight face. Just as he smoothed the surface of his life with lies, so too did he keep a composed face, an unruffled demeanor, even when his anxieties and fears were greatest.

At the moment his anxieties and fears were abating. What gave him comfort was the practical reminder that Charlotte hated office parties, hadn't been near one in at least two years. Charlotte steered clear of the office. She journeyed to New York with reluctance, and then only for reasons associated with her painting. Moreover, he now asked himself with a confident smile, what if she and Lorimer *did* happen to meet? What could she say—that she had heard he was a supercilious bastard with waiters? Eyes still closed, Howard chuckled. When he considered it realistically, he knew there was no more chance of Charlotte checking up with Lorimer than there was that she would check up with the Yankee Stadium turnstile crew on whether he had been out to the ball game.

At this reassuring thought, his muscle tone seemed a little firmer. He began to relax.

Three-quarters of an hour later, he opened his eyes and looked from the window to see the dim cavernous aspect of Grand Central Terminal and its gloomy passenger platform. Sitting up straight, unfolding his jacket, he glanced about the car—and counted no fewer than ten guys slouched low in their seats, newspapers folded on their laps, faces slack, still cherishing these last few seconds of repose and convalescence before the train jolted to a halt.

With a feeling of automation and renewed well-being, Howard made his way from the terminal out into the bright summer sunlight, walking with the swift-walking crowds. In another few minutes he had made it to the huge glass and black-marble edifice that had been his home away from home for nearly two decades, the world headquarters of NSA, an enormous electronics corporation which managed each and every year to sell, as Howard sometimes drolly remarked, far more electronic equipment than necessary. It was the sort of *mot* he was fond of making. Somehow it reduced life to a droll level, where he could feel at home with it. Taking life seriously made him uncomfortable—for despite his unruffled composure, he was a man whose self-esteem was held together with Scotch tape.

Howard revolved with the revolving door.

✳ two

His trajectory carried him first to the lobby news stand for two packs of cigarettes, thence running and skidding along a marble floor to catch an automatic elevator whose door was about to close. Shouldering the door, he slipped in and rode up to the eighth floor where, as the day progressed, he would discharge the modest duties inherent in his modest job.

When Howard was younger, upon first recognizing that he was going nowhere in life, and that he would never be one of the great men of his time, he had taken the trouble to console himself. He took note of various great men of his time, those who had worked long and hard and risen to be presidents and cabinet members—only to be shot down by critics intent upon placing them in historical perspective, whereupon after leaving office they lived out their declining years reading in newspapers and magazines how mediocre they had been. Where were all the father figures? And why try to be one when in the end they were so demolished, their private lives whispered about, their financial dealings questioned—and when nearly always they were accused of heavy contributions to the truth-and-honesty gap?

For his part, Howard had served for many years as editor of his company's house organ, a magazine known as *The Electron*, which was distributed to every employee of NSA, not only to those in the New York office but to those in the Chicago, Detroit, St. Louis, Memphis, Atlanta, and Los Angeles offices. Each wholesaler distributing NSA products received five copies and each retail outlet received three. The magazine went out unsolicited—no one had ever been known to buy a copy. Once published quarterly, it now came out only twice a year.

Since putting out two issues a year hardly kept Howard busy, he had recently become the sole member of a department called Special Assignments, which, like the magazine, was under the direct supervision of Malcolm Lorimer, president of the company. Howard's special assignments were relatively few and tended to be repetitive. Occasionally he was sent to the Memphis and Atlanta offices for sales meetings or dinner with some branch executive, but for the past several months he had had no special assignments whatever except for those he assigned himself.

For a liar, for a man leading a complex life, what Howard had at NSA was an ideal job. It was secure, it paid decently, it afforded convenient cover-stories and it was highly relaxing, often as relaxing as the train rides. So light were his editorial and special assignment duties that, unbeknownst to Malcolm Lorimer, he was even able to do a little moonlighting, which took the form of selling real estate on weekends, in the vicinity of Welton. To Howard, this real estate activity was important, for his commissions provided him with what he regarded as "extra" money and it was this money, unaccounted for to Charlotte, which he spent upon his extramarital pursuits. Sadie Fitch and her predecessors were luxuries which he could have otherwise hardly afforded, except by cutting into the standard of living he gave Charlotte, and at this he drew the line.

That morning, as he approached the glassed-in cubicle that served as his office, he saw that June Priestley, his new secretary, was doing a crossword puzzle in the slightly smaller cubicle across the aisle from his own. June had been with him less than two weeks and there was something about her that he found vaguely disturbing, perhaps merely the fact that she was so uncommunicative. He knew she had been in psychoanalysis for years and recently had progressed to what she spoke of as Group Therapy. Beyond this, he knew very little. A slender girl with hollow eyes and long dark hair, she clothed her angularity nearly always in black, at first a black blouse and skirt, then for almost a full week a black pants-suit. Today she was again wearing the blouse and skirt, the latter quite short.

As Howard passed by, June smiled faintly and re-crossed her legs, watching his face closely to see if he had looked at her legs when she re-crossed them, which he had. To his puzzlement, it struck him that she had crossed her legs not in the service of seduction but merely to study his reaction.

Feeling abruptly like a lab case but offering her a nonthe-less cheery good morning, Howard entered his office, hung up his jacket, loosened his tie, slumped down at his desk, lit a cigarette and yawned. Wearily he glanced at the morning mail, which looked inconsequential save for a large brown envelope which he knew would contain a water color he had commissioned at Lorimer's suggestion for the cover of the next issue, due out nearly five months hence, just before the end of the year. In putting out a magazine with an electronic motif, it was necessary to stretch the imagination a bit, and often the connection of content with electronics seemed a bit forced, especially since Lorimer continually pressed for a na-tionalistic slant as well. Yawning again, giving his head a vigorous shake, Howard slit the envelope. The painting was of the barren west—electronic cables stretching over the prairies in the foreground toward mountain ranges in the background, and disappearing into infinity, presumably some-where in the vicinity of Colorado. It was good enough but Charlotte could have done better, and he would remember to tell her so.

Howard studied the painting, held it close, yawned, held it away, and called to June for coffee. At the sound of his voice, she ripped something from her typewriter, causing the roller to give forth a high-pitched scream. From this he judged that she had been typing a personal letter.

When she returned with his coffee, Howard settled down to the day's routine, sipping his coffee, smoking, glancing once again at the water color and then sifting through the rest of the mail, most of which was disposable. He now began to dispose of it—crumpling up one piece after another, taking careful aim and tossing them at the trash basket, which he kept not under his desk where it could be easily reached, but across the room, against the wall, where it was a tougher shot. Having run out of trash mail, he withdrew some unused, pristine sheets of bond letterhead from his desk drawer, squeezed them into wads, and continued to throw at the basket. Now he could be heard to mutter, ". . . five for seven . . . six for eight . . . hell, six for nine . . . *hell*, six for *ten* . . ."

When the muttering stopped and the last shot had been taken, June Priestley strode into his office, stooped to retrieve the wads that had missed, and dropped them into the trash basket. Then, looking at him without expression, she strode out again.

With target practice over, Howard turned his attention to the morning paper, which he had of course failed to read on the train because he had spent virtually the entire trip with his eyes closed.

Until now it had been a routine office morning and it remained routine until noon, when June left for lunch. Once she was gone, Howard began to pry. Normally he was not given to prying but he was mystified by her silence, her refusal to open up, the deadpan way she looked at him, and in the past few days he had begun to pry about her desk for some clue to her personality. In her top drawer there was nothing but the same Holiday Inn match folder that had been there all week. On her desk, along with a dictionary and thesaurus, she kept some books on abnormal behavior. His eye fell upon a volume entitled *The Sensuous Woman,* which had not been there the day before. He pulled it out, leafed through it, closed it— and then opened it again and sank slowly into June's secretarial posture-chair, still reading. Twenty minutes later, just before June was due back, he snapped it shut, replaced it in its slot and left for lunch, thinking of Sadie.

NSA was a corporation which somehow made immense profits while at the same time preserving, at least in its New York office, an atmosphere of measured dignity and calm. It was a place where no one seemed to work very hard. Among those who did not work very hard were Howard and his secretary, June Priestley. One who did was Malcolm Lorimer, a sturdy little man with a will of steel and a thousand eyes. Now just past sixty, Lorimer was renowned for energy, rectitude and idealism. It was his professed hope to create an island of decency and courtesy in a city of surliness and sin.

Having no luncheon appointment that day, Howard ate upstairs in the company cafeteria, a magnificent emporium reminiscent of the grand ballroom of a luxury hotel, complete with crystal chandeliers, Georgian panelling and excellent food at paternalistically low prices. Wandering in search of an empty space, he sat down finally with three members of the sales department. About ready to leave, they were exchanging quips about their selling experience and Howard listened without interest, laughing when they laughed. After they were gone, he sat munching the remainder of his sandwich, glancing now and then in the direction of Lorimer, who was poring over a sheaf of papers, seated alone directly beneath a chandelier. His hair was as white as his soul and his face was ruddy, winter and summer. When Howard looked at him, he sometimes thought of his lungs, and of the healthy pink tissue of which they must surely be composed.

Spotting Howard, Lorimer waved and Howard waved back, feeling important. He knew that Lorimer was very fond of him, perhaps because he managed to be a yes-man in an unexcited low-key way, employing the same tone and the same casual mannerisms he used when lying to Charlotte. When he visited Lorimer's office, instead of sitting tensely and deferentially upright as so many did, he tended to slump in his chair, letting his legs stick out carelessly and sometimes lacing his hands behind his head and yawning. He knew that over the years he had done a thorough job of ingratiating himself with Lorimer, and he supposed the ultimate reason was that instead of treating Lorimer as a tin god he treated him as just another guy, and Lorimer respected him for it.

That day, along with reading the newspaper and throwing wads of paper at the trash basket, Howard had a job function to perform. It concerned the water color that had come in the morning mail. At 3:00 that afternoon he carried it upstairs for Lorimer's perusal.

There was significance in the hour. Lorimer normally took a siesta from one to three and in this way augmented the energy that drove him early and late.

"Hi," Howard said with a grin. "That water color finally came in and I thought you might like to have a look. I've been studying it all morning, looking at it every which-way."

Placing the painting on Lorimer's desk, Howard stood back and waited. Lorimer bent forward, planting a clenched bronzed fist on either side of the painting. Widowed at fifty-five, Lorimer thereafter observed deep mourning for a long while but in recent years he had come out of it. Today, with his customary dark suit, he wore a fancy vest with gold-and-green vertical stripes and gold buttons, which gave him a natty appearance, even downright sportive.

Awaiting Lorimer's reaction, Howard slouched against the

wall, then moved to the window and looked out upon the nearby skyscrapers, blurred by the haze of the August humidity.

Lorimer always took a long time with everything. Still intent upon the painting, he raised first one loose fist and then the other, letting each fall in turn upon the desk. A man who would clench his fists in that manner, Howard thought, was probably capable of a supercilious and even cruel attitude toward some hapless waiter. All in a flash he saw himself and Lorimer at dinner together the previous evening. *The waiter stood respectfully by, pencil stub poised. Lorimer looked at him with irritation. He waggled his fingers in a curt gesture of dismissal. "We'll let you know when we're ready to order, Boris," he snapped. Boris slunk away.*

Well, it could have been like that, Howard told himself. It could have happened just that way, and how was Charlotte to know?

His thoughts were abruptly terminated by a question from Lorimer:

"Howard, how about having dinner with me tonight?"

Howard hesitated.

"I have something I'd like to talk over," Lorimer said. "Come back up here about five-thirty and we'll leave together. How about it? Can you make it?"

"Sure," Howard said thoughtfully. "I'd like to very much."

A less skilled liar, one less confident of his powers, might have felt a trace of panic at this point but Howard was sure he could handle whatever had to be handled.

Back downstairs, he sat alertly at his desk, thinking.

Reaching an impasse, he plucked a nail clipper from his desk drawer and carefully clipped his fingernails, all ten of them.

What seemed certain, as well as confusing, was that he absolutely should not tell his wife he was having dinner with his boss that night—even though he was.

What to tell her instead was the problem.

On his desk there was a phone message scrawled by June. The message said that he was to call George Urquhardt, a midtown photographer to whom he occasionally gave assignments and who, he was certain, was calling with the hope of scooping more business out of *The Electron*. It was a pitch Urquhardt made periodically.

Giving the message hardly a glance, Howard dialed Charlotte.

"Charlotte . . . Listen, I'm afraid I won't be home for dinner. Yes, I realize. I had every intention of being there, and I'm sorry . . . Well, can't you save them for tomorrow night? Well, I don't know what to say then because I've gotten myself all hung up with George Urquhardt . . . the photographer . . . the guy we use for the magazine. Urquhardt. *Urquhardt.* Hell, I don't know, what difference does it make? U-r-q-u-h-a-r-d-t . . . I think. He wants me to have dinner with him. He's threatening to raise his rates, damn him . . . Yeah, that's right, dollars and cents, always dollars and cents, good God what a world we live in. So I'll be eating in town. I won't be late."

As Howard hung up, the phone rang and he heard June answer it, heard her say, "Okay, I'll tell him."

Howard tore open his cigarette pack to get at the last cigarette. He crumpled the pack and took a shot, missing badly.

June came in. "Do you realize you're supposed to be having dinner with Mr. Lorimer?"

Obviously she had overheard his conversation with Charlotte. "Yes, June," he said calmly. "I realize it."

June looked puzzled. "Well, his secretary just called. He's changed his mind."

"*What?*"

"Instead of coming up to his office, you're supposed to meet him at the restaurant."

"Oh."

"Here's the address." June put a slip of paper before him. "What's wrong, Mr. Carew? You look as if you're having an identity crisis." Picking up the cigarette pack from the floor, she dropped it into the basket and left.

Howard frowned. He hadn't liked her nuances. Before he could decide what to do about it, she had returned and stood before his desk, looking intense. "Mr. Carew, there's something I simply must say to you," she said. "I can't let it go by any longer."

Howard took out his nail clipper and began clipping his nails again. "What's that, June?"

She sat on the corner of his desk. He looked up briefly, and then back at his nails. She was certainly a hollow-eyed girl, he thought. The flesh under her eyes was certainly a lot darker than her cheeks. Maybe if she were not so intense she would not look so hollow-eyed. Or maybe if she were not so hollow-eyed she would not look so intense.

"First of all," she said, "this job isn't anything very great to me. I can get a job anywhere. Okay? So I'm unafraid. I'm freed up." She looked up from the floor. "I think that's something you should know, okay?"

Howard nodded. "I've got a feeling you're trying to tell me something, June."

"Yep . . . but I'm having second thoughts. Maybe this isn't the time or place. I've changed my mind. It's something we should have a vista of time for."

Howard looked up from his nails and frowned.

"I'll tell you what, Mr. Carew. Maybe you could buy me a drink some night after work—I realize, of course, that you have a very tight schedule." The leer was unmistakable. "But it's very important to me that we talk. So please try and fit me in. Tomorrow evening after work maybe?"

Howard nodded. "Can I let you know?"

"Of course," she said, walking slowly out. "Of course."

Howard replaced the nail clipper. He drummed on the desk, hurting his fingertips. He picked up the phone. Although it was true that he had planned to go home for dinner, it was equally true that he had promised Sadie he would stop by Barney's Tavern on his way to the train. Between acting jobs, Sadie worked as a waitress, which meant that she worked as a waitress most of the time. She was currently working at Barney's Tavern.

He dialed Barney's and waited while she was called to the phone. "Hi," he said. "Listen, I'm very sorry but something has come up. I can't make it."

"I under-*stand*," she said in a small voice.

"I'm sorry."

"It's perfectly all right, I understand, I really do."

"I'll call you when I—get clear."

"Okay. Good night, darling. And please be careful. Will you be carrying your gun?"

"I'm not sure."

"Well please be careful."

"I will," Howard said. "I promise."

"Do you promise?"

"Yes. I promise."

Howard hung up. He took out his secret checkbook and examined the balance—the balance he fed with his real estate commissions. It was getting low. He sighed.

A few minutes before five, June called, "Mr. Carew, have you been reading my *Sensuous Woman* by any chance?"

"Your what?" Howard's voice contained a note of mystification—put there by Howard. When June didn't reply, he called again, "Your *what*, June?"

"Never mind," she called back.

Dinner with Lorimer was notable for a number of reasons beyond the sheer fact that he was indeed having dinner with Lorimer. For one thing, right from the outset, he noticed Lorimer's kindly attitude toward their waiter. The restaurant he had chosen was Italian, and it was one which Lorimer obviously patronized frequently. He was well known to the head waiter, to the waiter who served them, and even to the busboys. With a concern that was clearly sincere, he asked their waiter about the health of his mother who, it turned out, had been suffering from arthritis.

One reason he had asked Howard to dinner, Lorimer said, was to discuss an idea he had for expanding the range of articles which they might use for the magazine. In a narrow sense, he explained, articles on electronics offered little freedom of choice in subject matter, as they both had discovered over the years. He proposed an ever-broadening base.

"For instance, Howard," he said, "how about an article on Chesapeake Bay fishing boats?"

"Chesapeake Bay fishing boats?"

"Party boats." Lorimer's eyes briefly showed impatience. "I'm quite serious about this. You may not think much of it, but the fact is that all those fellows nowadays have two-way radios and they talk back and forth to each other about where the fish are and whether they're catching any and so forth. And most of them are equipped with sonar detectors so they get a blip on their screens when fish are about. What do you think?"

Howard said he thought it was an extremely imaginative idea.

"Good," Lorimer said. "Now then. I have a special assignment for you. I'm due in Los Angeles the last week of September, and I'd like very much for you to go in my place. You'd need to be there by the night of Wednesday, September twenty-fifth. Will that be convenient for you, Howard?"

Howard said he thought it would.

"Our Los Angeles people are having a three-day workshop and I'm supposed to make a speech," Lorimer said. "I'd like you to make it for me." Lorimer grinned. In spite of his white hair, he looked far younger than his years, perhaps because he was so healthy and ruddy. He was still grinning. "Don't worry," he said, "it's all written, Howard. All you have to do is read it—on my behalf."

"Right," Howard said. He found the assignment appealing. His mind was working in its customary channels. "I'll be happy to," he said.

"You could fly back the next day," Lorimer said. "Or if you prefer you can stay out there for a few days and take in the workshop, it's entirely up to you."

Howard's horizons were expanding.

"Just let my secretary know when you'd like your return plane reservation," Lorimer said." Maybe . . . you'd like to have your wife go with you . . ."

Howard nodded, as if thinking it over. "I doubt it seriously," he said. "She's not much for plane travel. Gets airsick."

"Well, just whatever you wish. I know that some wives don't enjoy being left at home. Mine never did . . ." Thoughtfully Lorimer sipped his coffee. His eyes had a faraway look. "My wife has been dead five years this past week. It seems impossible that it could be that long. It takes time to adjust to the loss of a wife."

Howard nodded sympathetically. "I know I'd hate to lose mine," he said, and it was true. His life was a carefully worked out equation in which Charlotte was a vital component.

Lorimer seemed lost in reverie, gazing across the room toward a huge oil painting of Venice that hung on a square of black velvet. "Well . . ." With grave courtesy he asked the waiter for the check. "I'm so glad we had this opportunity, Howard. Having dinner together, the two of us, is something that's been on my mind for a long time."

Howard nodded. "It's something I've thought about a good deal too," he said.

Lorimer left handsome tips for one and all, and they were bowed out as if they were visiting royalty or television personalities.

At breakfast next morning in Connecticut, Howard told Charlotte that George Urquhardt had a bastardly attitude about dollars and cents, accusing him of unseemly avarice with little regard for the quality of his workmanship, an attitude which, he went on, was becoming increasingly prevalent in the United States and doubtless in the world at large. He also accused Urquhardt of having a penchant for cheap gin as well as a gluttonous addiction to Roquefort dressing, describing how he had scooped great gobs of it onto his salad.

He then drove off to the depot, thinking of his trip to Los Angeles.

✳ three

At 4:30 that evening, June Priestley asked permission to leave the office early. At 5:30 he met her at a bar of her own selection, one she had obviously chosen for its obscurity and its dim lighting.

What June had done was go home and get dressed, and although it was so dark that he couldn't see very well, he liked what he could see. She wore a dark blouse and a very short white skirt, hardly more than a valance. They sat on bar-stools and her face was a pale mask, with her long hair merging into the darkness.

Howard ordered a martini for himself and she asked for ginger ale.

For one who had been so uncommunicative, June now seemed hell-bent upon communicating. "Okay now, Mr. Carew," she said crisply. "I'm coming straight to the point. I don't consider this a date."

"There's no danger," Howard said. "If anybody from the office comes in they won't be able to see us unless they've got night vision."

"Your eyes will get accustomed to it," she said. "Okay, here we go . . ."

"Okay, June, so what's the point?"

"The point is that you're a big liar, Mr. Carew, that's the point."

Howard by now was sipping his martini. He swallowed carefully and set his glass on the bar. "Good God!"

June was silent for a few moments, as if to allow time for

the point to sink in. She sipped her ginger ale, looking calmly straight ahead. "Do you remember a night about two weeks ago?"

"*What* night about two weeks ago?"

"I think it was only about my second or third day on the job, right after I'd started to work for you. We bumped into each other on Third Avenue . . . after work."

Howard nodded. "Oh, yeah . . ."

"You asked me where I was headed and I said I was going to my Group Therapy session. You said you were on your way home, and then something about having a drink with an old friend from Newport News . . ."

Howard nodded. "So?"

"You left," June said, "and I walked on. I remember all this so clearly for a particular reason. About a block later I stopped. I found myself looking in a window at a black negligee—and all of a sudden it came over me. I said to myself, Mr. Carew is a big liar. I just knew it, and it had only taken me two or three days, or whatever it was, to find out."

Howard sipped his martini. "Why? How?"

"Don't ask me. I just knew it. And for a while I was worried about myself."

"About *yourself?*"

"Yes. Because of the black negligee, you see. I was standing there looking at a black negligee, and all of a sudden I was thinking of you. I had to ask myself if there was any significance in the coincidence. My doctor says the possibility of hidden significance should never be discounted."

"I see." From long habit, and perhaps because he now thought it might be a good idea, Howard turned suave. In a calculated way he glanced at her short white skirt and her black stockings. The visibility was getting better. Perched as she was on the high stool, when she crossed her legs, as she had just done, the skirt rode high and wide. She had better legs than he had thought. "So what did you decide?" he murmured.

"I decided there was no significance whatever. It was the way you said what you said about the guy from Newport News."

Howard shook his head. "What the hell, June—"

"How on earth did you pick Newport News?"

"What's wrong with Newport News? A lot of people have friends from Newport News."

She was smiling. "Okay, that's not important. It was the way you said it. I knew I was right, so I set out to prove it to myself. And boy, have I proved it!"

"How have you proved it?"

"Okay, let's take yesterday. You never close your door and when you get excited you talk very loud. I heard you on the phone telling your wife that you were having dinner with George Urquhardt, right? Instead you were having dinner with Mr. Lorimer, as we both know. Why were you ashamed of having dinner with Mr. Lorimer? What's he—some kind of B-girl?"

Howard chuckled. "Now listen, June . . ."

"And *yet* . . ." She shook her head helplessly. "On at least three different occasions I've heard you telling your wife on the phone that you *were* having dinner with Lorimer —once when I knew for a fact that Mr. Lorimer was in Los Angeles. And all three times—" June repressed a smile. "Not that I think it's funny, as you'll soon see—but all three times, after hanging up, you come strolling across to my office, yawning and stretching and saying something like, 'Well, quite a day, huh, June?' or 'Well, it's a crazy life, huh, June?' Something philosophical that goes with yawning and stretching. It's a dead giveaway."

Howard looked at his empty glass then held it aloft so the bartender could see it. "Very observant, aren't you?"

"Yes, I am. Like yesterday, when I asked you whether you'd been into my copy of *The Sensuous Woman*. I knew you had, you see. Because when I came back from lunch I found it slightly out of place. You see, I have a thing. I alway make sure that my books are lined up very precisely, never uneven by the slightest hair. I realize it's a compulsion and I realize I'm indulging it, but my doctor says it's not harmful so long as I know why I do it."

"Why do you do it?"

"It's a form of fetishism, linked up inversely with superstition and all tied in with the kind of a housekeeper my mother was, but that's not the point."

"What *is* the point?"

"The point is, Mr. Carew, that I have no wish to be secretary to a dishonest person."

Calmly Howard grabbed up the martini the bartender had set before him.

"Honesty is just too important to me, it really is. I've spent too many years and too much money to become the kind of person I've become . . . to let dishonesty pass. If I let it pass, if I disregard it, then I become something I don't like at all."

Howard nodded, looking again at her legs.

"I could mention other things," she said. "The way you keep wadding up paper and throwing it at the trash basket. I can hear you in there muttering, 'Okay, now, Walt Frazier, okay this time Bill Bradley, okay now the butcher.' "

Howard laughed. "DeBusschere. So what's wrong with that?"

"There's nothing *wrong* with it. But it shows something a little peculiar in your makeup. As far as I'm concerned it contributes to an overall picture of a disturbed man."

"I don't feel disturbed." Howard laughed again.

"You wouldn't think it was so funny if you could have heard what our Group said about it last week."

"Your Group? What Group?"

"Our Group Therapy Group."

Abruptly Howard set down his glass. "Do you mean to tell me . . . that at your Group Therapy meetings . . . you talk about *me* . . . throwing wads of paper . . . at the *trash* basket?"

"Of course. We talk about everything."

"Well my good God almighty." Howard gulped his martini. "What *did* your Group say about me last week?"

"Don't you know about Groups, Mr. Carew? We talk about the most intimate details of our lives. Dr. Denison encourages it. That's the way Groups work. We display our hostility and everything. We're his advanced patients, you see."

"You still haven't told me what your Group said about *me* last week."

"I guess I'd rather not tell you."

"Okay, don't." Howard took another gulp and slid from his stool. "Pardon me, I have to go to the bathroom." He started off and turned back. "Why can't you tell me?"

"I'd just rather not."

"Okay, then don't." He took a couple of steps and again turned back. "I think you'd better tell me."

"I think maybe you'd better go to the bathroom before it's too late." June was smirking.

"I'll be the judge of that," Howard said with dignity. He walked a steady course to the men's room. When he returned, he drained his glass and asked, "What are you trying to tell me, June? That you want to quit?"

"You're looking at my legs, Mr. Carew. No, I don't want to quit. Do you want to know one big reason why I don't want to quit? Because of what I'd have to tell the Personnel Office. See? I told you it wasn't funny."

Howard felt some of his dignity drain away. All in a flash

he had glimpsed June marching up to Personnel, announcing that she had to quit because her principles did not permit her to work for a liar. Then he saw the Director of Personnel relaying this information to Malcolm Lorimer. Howard closed his eyes.

"You see, Mr. Carew," June was saying. "I feel I can help you. I don't believe in the notion of collective guilt, and that's where I differ from some of my peer group. I don't condemn your whole generation as a lump."

Howard withdrew his attention from the Director of Personnel and returned it to June. "That's nice," he said.

"I feel that if each one of *us* took one of *you*—and really set out to help you—it would be the compassionate thing to do."

Howard looked about for the bartender.

"Instead of simply scorning you," she said. "Just leaving you out to die."

"Can I have another martini before I die?" He signalled for one.

"You persist in thinking it's funny," she said. "You see, the easy way out for me would be simply to quit and get it over with. But I'd rather try to help you, and I feel I can. If you'll let me. Don't be worried. I could never make a physical commitment to you."

Howard winced. "Who in the hell asked you to?"

"This is your third martini," June said as it was placed before him. "After you finish this one, we leave. I have to meet Hank."

"Who's Hank?"

"Hank and I live together."

"Are you and Hank planning to get married?"

She laughed. "You can't be serious. Poor Hank. Have him end up like you? All hung up? Lying his life away?" She put her hand on his sleeve. "You should be worried about yourself, Mr. Carew, you really should. Lying is self-destructive. It can become pathological. With you, it may already be pathological. Come on now, drink it, don't nurse it."

Howard took a gulp.

"I have something I'd like you to read." June opened her purse and handed him some folded sheets from a magazine. "Read it on the way home," she said.

Howard struck a match and tried to read. The match went out.

"Read it on the train." As she slid from her stool, Howard took the rest of his martini at a gulp. "Thanks so much for the ginger ale," she said.

Howard grunted.

Laughing, she patted his arm. "You're worth saving," she said. "What interests me—what *fascinates* me—is that you don't think so."

"*I?* Don't think *I'm* worth saving?"

"That's right," June said. "Night." She was gone.

Howard waited until the train cleared Grand Central and was rolling through the night. Then he unfolded the sheets June had given him and read:

"A pathological liar may be defined as one whose lying is so compulsive and habitual as to constitute a form of mental disease."

Frowning, he read on:

"Pathological liars deliver their lies with ease and confidence. They deny misconduct with nonchalance. Their lies are often imaginative, often quite elaborate. Having told a lie, they will go to great lengths to support it."

Howard began to mutter.

"A pathological liar falls under the general heading of sociopath. Sociopaths are constantly in trouble, do not profit from experience, tend to have no genuine loyalties."

He knew he had genuine loyalties—to Charlotte, among others.

"They are callous, egocentric, emotionally immature and irresponsible. More often than not, they are extremely vain."

Howard involuntarily touched his hairpiece.

"Sociopaths include addicts—persons who are addicted to alcohol, drugs, etc. They also include sexual deviates—those embracing homosexuality, flagellism, masochism, fetishism, bestiality, satyriasis and the like."

Howard pressed his nose to the window. The cool glass felt soothing.

"Satyriasis is a term applied solely to males (in females: nymphomania) and used to designate an excessive or insatiable desire for sexual gratification. There are men who indulge in sexual relations as much as several times a day for long periods."

Howard's eyebrows went up.

"The question is why this impulse occurs so excessively. The answer lies not in the sexual desire itself but rather in some inner need. One satyr may need constant reassurance of potency; another may fear latent homosexuality; a third may be warding off anxiety, or escaping from home or business problems; a fourth may be compensating for feelings of failure or frustration; some satyrs, homely or socially inept, may be attempting to prove they are attractive to women."

Howard looked at his reflection, blurred by the dirty window.

"A case history of Norman S."

He then read the case of the unfortunate Norman S., an overweight salesman, who was so thoroughly preoccupied with copulation that it interfered with his sales work. He knew that if he didn't cut it out soon he would lose his job, which he not only liked but badly needed. He sought treatment and —after a brief final spurt of redoubled activity—began to make good progress and in a year was cured. "Thus was a good job retained," the case history noted.

Howard read on. "Withdrawal symptoms: Milder effects include vague uneasiness, headaches and depression."

Milder effects?

He shook his head, imagining what the others might be. He sat there disgusted, calling June a crazy little doctrinaire bitch, and then plunged onward, reading of the various degrees of affliction and of the varying responses of individual patients to different types of therapy.

At last he folded the article twice and dropped it to the floor. Then he stepped on it.

Presently he shoved it with his foot up under the seat of the man sitting in front of him.

✳ four

There were times when Howard accused himself of being the worst person in the world, the most thoroughly worthless, the most outrageously deceitful. After telling himself these things he always felt a great deal better. He felt a sense of release which enabled him to carry on with the worthless life in question.

Next morning on the train he told himself how worthless he was, and with this out of the way he began to think in practical terms. Thinking of June and of the danger she posed to his way of life, he persuaded himself that she posed none whatever. In the cold light of morning he found it impossible to believe that she would execute a threat of any kind. She was merely being self-important.

He decided to treat the whole matter lightly.

When he reached the office she was there ahead of him, looking once more like somebody in deep mourning, with her black bellbottoms, black blouse, hair pulled back and tied with a black ribbon. "Hi ya, June," he said lightly.

"Good morning." She followed him into his office and sat on the edge of his desk. "Coffee?"

Howard shrugged. "I'm no satyr, I know that much."

"Would you like me to go down for coffee?"

"I'm no sociopath either."

June nodded. "Where's my article?"

"Have you told Personnel on me yet?"

She smiled and slipped from the desk. "Do you have my article?"

"No, I left it on the train. I'm sorry. I didn't realize you wanted it back."

"It's okay," she said. "I mean, I think it's good you're being truthful. You could have said the wind blew it away or something . . . Coffee?"

"Please."

Although he was determined to take June lightly, he found very soon that office life was no longer quite the same. In mid-morning, as he dialed Sadie's number, he looked up to see June. Holding a wad of paper between thumb and forefinger, she was sighting downward at the trash basket, as if she were a bombardier. On the second ring, Howard hung up. June let the wad of paper go and it fell into the basket.

"June . . ."

"Yes?" She turned with a smile.

"Is there something wrong with your trash basket?"

"No."

"If there is, I can have Supply bring up a new one."

"No need."

"I'm going to start closing the door."

She left, and Howard sat there frowning. For the first time it occurred to him that she might be serious. Half an hour later he crossed the hall to her office. "On the subject of lying . . ." he began. "Just academically . . ."

She looked up from her dictionary. "Yes?"

"A person can often lie out of kindness. The truth can be very hurtful."

Her eyes went back to the dictionary. "The opposite is true —in both cases."

Howard looked down at the crown of her head. It gave him pleasure to note that she had a little dandruff. He perched himself on the edge of her desk. "I enjoyed last night," he said.

"Did you? Did you *really?*"

"Yes, I did. Really." He picked up her hand and held it briefly. "You have very nice hands, June. Do you realize that?"

Her eyes were dancing. "Thanks, Mr. Carew."

"You also have very nice legs." Howard got up. "I don't see why you persist in hiding them—in those damned things." June started laughing. "What's funny?"

She shook her head, still smiling. He glanced down at the dictionary. "What word are you looking up?"

" 'Odious.' I'm just building my vocabulary." She was still smiling. "This is such a nice job, Mr. Carew. It's so totally relaxing."

"It won't always be like this. After I finish the July issue we always have a lull."

"How long will the lull last?"

"Until about the first of October."

"That's a very nice lull," June said. "Gosh, it's true that I'm not dependent upon it—but who in her right mind would want to give up a job like *this?*"

"Don't even consider it."

"But Mr. Carew," she said, quite gravely now. "I really wish you'd give some serious thought to what I was saying last night. Otherwise I'll have no choice . . ."

"June, I think you'll find your fears about me are very exaggerated. Just enjoy your job, okay? *Okay?*"

June smiled.

He waited until she had gone out to lunch, then called Sadie again. "Thank God," Sadie breathed. "You're alive."

Howard chuckled. "I'll be at Barney's tonight."

"Oh, boy!"

Howard hung up, savoring the sound of her voice when she said, "Oh, boy!" He then called Charlotte to tell her he would not be home for dinner. Charlotte did not answer. After trying her twice more, he went out to lunch and while he was out he tried without success to call her from a phone booth. In the city of New York, vandalizing telephones was very much in vogue, and Howard walked six blocks on and about Madison Avenue, trying one public phone after another and finding them all garrotted.

Finally he returned from lunch and as the afternoon progressed, so too did his irritation. "By God," he muttered, "If every time I call my own wife, I have to sneak out of my own office—and go find a public telephone—I refuse."

A few minutes later he rode the elevator down to the lobby and called Charlotte from a booth that was partially obscured by the newsstand. The line was busy. He tried twice more and twice more it was busy. Resisting the urge to crack the mouthpiece against the coin box, he went back upstairs.

June said that Charlotte was on the line, waiting.

"Hi," he said. "I've been trying to get you—to say I won't be home for dinner."

"Traynor's office called," Charlotte replied. Her voice was conspiratorial, a near-whisper. "Captain Traynor's in Maine on vacation and somebody else is out sick and they want you to show a house this evening." Charlotte was trained to be close-mouthed about his real estate activity. "His secretary said it was very important, a hot prospect."

"Okay, thanks, I'll take care of it. Well, in any case just forget about me for dinner. I'll pick up something somewhere—and be home when I get home. Okay?"

Charlotte seemed unconcerned. Howard hung up and sat at his desk, thinking. There was little he found so challenging as a seemingly insoluble problem in logistics, a problem involving deadlines and tight scheduling and split-second timing in travel arrangements. His secret checking account was low —he could not pass up the opportunity to make a sale. Yet he hated the thought of not seeing Sadie. To handle both seemed an impossible challenge, but for that very reason it appealed to him enormously. He liked feeling that time was short. He liked running late. It gave him a sense of urgency, and of knowing his arrival was being awaited.

In his role as part-time realtor, Howard worked through a firm known as Venture Realty, run by an old reprobate named Richard Traynor. It was his custom to make himself available if needed on Saturdays and Sundays and sometimes on week-nights if a crisis arose. There were also occasions when he would "sit on" a house that was listed for sale on an open-inspection basis.

Tingling with determination, Howard telephoned Traynor's secretary and asked her to set up the appointment for 6:30. Leaving the office a little early, he rode the train out to

Westport, picked up his car at the depot parking lot, and drove off to Venture Realty.

The prospects were a young couple named Thompson, and as Traynor's secretary introduced them, Howard noted that they seemed awed. Both were blonde and both were very pale, as if they hadn't been out in the sun all summer.

The house he showed them stood squarely on the boundary line between an elite neighborhood and one that was modest and even a little shabby. From the state highway, the most direct approach led down a street lined with run-down houses. This was the approach that surely would be used by anyone living in the house once it was bought. On the listing card, for office eyes only, Captain Traynor had written, "approach house from good side." Through a series of deceitful zigzags that carried him eight blocks out of his way, Howard did as bidden, managing to convey the impression that the immediate neighborhood was composed exclusively of very expensive houses.

"It's a house where many happy hours have been spent," he said, leading the way to the front door.

The previous owner had committed suicide. The widow had it up for sale.

"I think you'll find that it's a good 'learning' house," Howard said as they stood in the kitchen.

"What's that mean?" The young wife laughed nervously, as if fearful that she might betray stupidity of some sort.

Howard hesitated. For some reason he found that he was not quite up to his usual standard of glibness. "Well, I mean it's a very good house for learning household skills," he said. "I mean particularly if you're just starting out in life. This house is a challenge—you wouldn't have to touch a thing if you didn't want to, but it's also a challenge—if you want to *make* it a challenge, do you see what I mean?"

The wife's eyes were wide and earnest. "I think I do," she said. "Gosh, I've never thought of it that way before." She turned to her husband. "Have you, Billy?"

"Are you handy with tools . . . Bill?" Howard asked.

"No sir, not very. Farm tools, but not much else."

"Well, with this house you'd learn to be." Howard found that he was listening to the sound of his own voice. "I mean, if you *wanted* to be, that is. It would be entirely up to you. This house could stay just as it is and you could be perfectly happy in it. But everything you did to it would of course raise its value by just that much."

"I think I see what Mr. Carew means, Billy," the wife said.

"It's like with a job," Howard said after a pause. "When you're young you take a job not for how much money it pays you but for how much it can teach you, at least that's the way I think a person *should* look at it."

Both nodded.

"Same way with a house, and this is the point I want to make. Start out with a house where you can really learn— about *houses*. About the plumbing and the electricity and a certain amount of structural background, some carpentry, maybe a little masonry—and then, when you're older and ready for a bigger, more expensive house, well—you're really ready for it."

"I never thought of it that way before," Mrs. Thompson said.

Howard shrugged. "You're not alone. A lot of people haven't. Believe you me."

They continued to trail through the house and he knew from experience that neither husband nor wife had what might be called a practiced eye, neither knew what to look for. Upstairs in the master bedroom, he saw young Mr. Thompson take his wife's hand. The sight of them holding hands did something to Howard that he hadn't expected. He found himself faltering—but from long years of habit he plunged ahead. "Are you folks new in Westport?" he asked as they followed him downstairs.

"Yes, we're from Ohio," Mr. Thompson said. "I'm with the Granite Insurance Company and I've been transferred from the Cleveland office to Hartford."

"Sounds like a promotion," Howard said.

"Indeed it is," Mrs. Thompson said with pride.

"Insurance is a very interesting business," Howard said. "There's certainly a lot—to it."

"Yes indeed there is," Mrs. Thompson said.

"It means commuting, of course," Mr. Thompson said. "But we were told that Westport was a nicer place to live than Hartford."

"Well . . ." Howard chuckled. "We in Westport think so."

"This is—what? Forty-nine thousand?"

"It's listed at forty-nine-five but—well, I just can't say. I think they'd listen to an offer, although I do know that she's already turned down a firm offer of forty-two."

The widow was in fact still considering a firm offer of thirty-nine-five.

"Our parents are going to help us with the down payment," Mrs. Thompson said.

"I see." Howard smiled. "Well, that's very nice. It gives a parent a great deal of pride to be able to offer a helping hand to somebody just getting started. That sort of thing means a great deal to a parent—would your parents like to have a look at the house?"

"Oh no, they're back in Ohio," Mrs. Thompson said. "They're leaving it strictly up to us."

"That's the ticket," Howard said. "I think that's the best way to foster a feeling of independence in kids. I admire it."

As they made the return trip, taking the same devious route

out that they had taken in, Mr. Thompson said, "Honey, I don't know about you but I kind of like what Mr. Carew here says about it being a good house to *learn* on. Somehow that impresses me."

Howard's thoughts were far away, his eyes were on the road. "Good boy, Bill," he said.

By the time he dropped the Thompsons off at the real estate office, it was 7:15. Still in his car, he headed for New York and by 8:40 he was sitting on a barstool in Barney's Tavern, gobbling a sandwich and sipping a martini.

That evening he found himself in a mood of somber quietude, which may have been brought on by sheer fatigue or possibly by a reaction to his handling of the young Thompsons. Lips parted, sandwich poised, he stared solemnly into the dark, highly versatile mirror which covered the wall behind the bar, the mirror all the drinkers on their stools might gaze into and find whatever reflection they wished. When he focussed upon his own blurred image, he saw heavy shoulders and a massive head. For the most part, however, his eyes were out of focus, giving him a faraway look which did not pass unnoticed.

It was noticed particularly by George the bartender, who was paying it due respect. At Barney's, Howard was a man of mystery. No one knew what he did. The consensus was that he was either a CIA agent or a narcotics agent—suppositions which Howard neither confirmed nor denied, thereby giving all the confirmation anyone might need. Even with Sadie, he firmly refused to tell what he did or where he lived, what his phone number was, or indeed anything about himself. From this she judged that his life was hazardous. To Sadie—and at Barney's—he was known as Howard Jefferson. Only a week or so earlier, it had given him pleasure to overhear George say in a low voice to another customer: "You name it—Mr. Jefferson's done it." George now doubtless was attributing Howard's present mood to weighty thoughts, important decisions—perhaps concern over a difficult international assignment, perhaps a mood of reminiscence over a past triumph.

"Well . . ." Howard drained off the rest of his martini, set down the glass in a decisive, mood-snapping way, and smiled at George, who thereupon asked with great respect, "Tough day, huh?"

For Howard, of course, it had indeed been a tough day. He spread his hands. "All days are tough in one way or another, aren't they, George?"

It was a remark of virtually no importance, yet because Howard had spoken it, George seemed to find it impressive. George was short, nearly bald and pink-cheeked. He was laying out olives on a napkin for quick pickup. By the thoughtful way George was lining up the olives, Howard could tell that he was impressed.

He gave George a reassuring smile, wanting to assure George that he liked him. Howard liked people, particularly the very young, the very old and the very short. When he did a kind act or said something nice he was so overcome with love for the object of his kindness, or possibly for himself, that he often choked up. Tears would come to his eyes, and he would be acutely aware of the glory of life.

Ordering another martini, he watched the flourishes George made as he mixed it, and then smiled indulgently as George, in placing it before him, slopped some on the bar. "Oops," George said. "Sorry."

"It's okay, George."

George got a rag, picked up the glass, wiped the bar very carefully, wiped the bottom of the glass and set it down again. "Very sorry, Mr. Jefferson," he said.

"Don't worry about it," Howard said.

George looked solemn. "I know," he said, "but something

like that can be very irritating to a customer, you know what I mean?"

"George . . ." Howard's smile was benign. "I don't think . . . frankly . . ." He felt a lump in his throat. ". . . that anything you could ever do would irritate me."

Howard could tell that George was warmed by what he had said, that it was a remark George would remember and probably even tell his wife about. It was a very nice thing he had said to George. Howard lowered his head over his martini. His eyes were misty. When he could see again, he glanced at his watch and peered toward the rear of the tavern, into the dim, orange-lit chambers where tables and booths accommodated diners. Presently he caught a glimpse of Sadie in her costume. What the waitresses wore at Barney's seemed more costume than uniform. They wore long beige skirts and laced bodices, giving an effect that was Hogarthian. George said Barney wanted them all to look like eighteenth-century milkmaids who were at all times only a customer's smile away from a hayloft. Sadie looked that way, even though she was far from robust. She had a fragile rib-cage and long blonde hair. It was 9:15. She would be off at 9:30.

Sadie's name was Sarah Elizabeth Fitch, and she came from a very small town in the Shenandoah Valley. At twenty-two she had come up to New York with the hope of starring in a Broadway musical. As the years passed, she lowered her sights. In the early years she slept around with almost any man who wanted her, and there were many who wanted her. At twenty-seven she had gotten married and then, after four months, was divorced. Now, at twenty-nine, she worked as a waitress, got an occasional commercial spot on television, and told Howard how important it was to her to have an older man in her life.

Sadie's appeal for Howard was her wistfulness. To him, she was a forlorn, beautiful ragamuffin, a poor little match girl who had been kicked around. To view her as a sad little girl brought out the very best in Howard. He came clattering out over the drawbridge in full mail, lance upthrust, pennon flying.

A few minutes before she was off duty, he went for his car and picked her up at the curb, fully expecting her to be sad about something because she almost invariably was. As they drove up York Avenue to her apartment, she gripped his hand very hard, saying nothing. Finally she sighed and took her hand away.

"What's wrong?" Howard asked. Of all the questions he asked her, it was the one he asked most frequently.

"I hate myself," she said.

"Don't say that, Sadie."

"I do. I hate myself."

"Why?"

"I'm a bitch."

"No you're not."

"Yes I am, I'm a bitch."

"Not to me, you're not."

"Well, I am to myself."

"Why do you say you're a bitch?"

"I just am."

Howard patted her head.

Once they were settled in bed in her darkened one-room apartment, Howard said, "I have something to ask you. How would you like to go to Los Angeles with me the last week in September?"

"Are you serious?"

"I have a Special Assignment out there," he said. "And I think I could work it if you can get a few days off."

"Gosh, Howard . . ."

"I couldn't be with you during the day, because I'll be—you know, kind of busy . . ."

"I understand."

"And I guess it would be best if we got on the plane separately, but we could sit together, of course . . ."

"Is it something dangerous?"

"Not really," he said. "At least not so far as I know."

"Will you have to carry your gun?"

"Not on the plane," he said. "They might think I was a hijacker."

Sadie laughed. "Of course."

"It's better if you don't ask too many questions," he said.

"I'm sorry."

"You understand."

"Yes, of course." She sighed. "Oh, Howard, that sounds too good to be true."

"I think if we're careful we can work it out."

"Oh, Howard . . ." Sadie turned to him and put her arms about his neck. "Howard, if I didn't have you, oh, God, if you only knew. I've been so depressed all day. Howard, please . . . I'm bruised . . . I've been beaten . . ."

While Howard made love to her, she kept speaking to him. When Howard replied at all, it was in monosyllables, since in the past year or so he had found himself short of breath and he needed to conserve it as best he could.

"You bought me, didn't you, Howard, and now you own me, don't you? I was lying on the dock, beaten, with my hands and feet tied and I had a smudge of dirt on my cheek and I was hoping that if somebody bought me it would be you. What year was it? What year was it, Howard? It was 1720, and I was dressed in burlap and I had silver fingernails and you bought me and took me on your ship, and I have this bed, this nice clean little bed that you let me have, and you keep me tied up all day long but every night you come down to my room and ravish me, don't you, Howard?"

"Yep," Howard said.

Howard dressed and drove home. Charlotte was asleep but she stirred when he got into bed. He murmured inanities about his clients, the young Thompsons, and of how guileless and unsophisticated they were and of how sorry he had felt for them. Charlotte mumbled something, turned over and soon was breathing rhythmically again, but for a long time Howard couldn't sleep.

∗ five

It was two days after the evening he spent with the young Thompsons and Sadie. The Thompsons had offered $42,500 and the widow gobbled it up. In spite of the commission he would get, Howard felt gloomy.

Holding his razor, he stood before the bathroom mirror and looked himself in the eye. As he did so he took some solace in noting the facial resemblance he bore to a noted pro football quarterback currently being featured in television after-shave commercials. The lather helped.

That evening he wore the close-fitting skin of Howard Carew, dependable burgher, attentive husband. With his wife, he went to dinner at the home of neighborhood friends, feeling part of the community, comfortable in his geologic layer. With the sobriety of a concerned citizen, he discussed gypsy moths, no trivial topic locally, for earlier in the summer the little bastards had gobbled up most of the foliage in town, turning bowers of greenery into naked spikes. In their larval state they worked high in the trees, chewing and chewing, spitting out what they didn't want, and the sound of the tiny leaf fragments falling on the forest floor was like the sound of light rain. Should the town have sprayed in advance, when it was known they were marching down from Mass.? The town had not. To spray, the town felt, would have been a clear betrayal of ecology. The argument waxed. Howard listened, drank, delivered safe, modest opinions.

His wife stood on the far side of the room. Her head was backlit by a floor lamp and her pale golden hair was soft from washing. She looked—he sought a word and came up with Impressionist. She was a French girl in a park, standing in a long dusty slant of afternoon sunlight, a girl with a slender neck, a puff of gold hair, and her eyes were pensive and wise. Against the talk of gypsy moths, he heard her say, "I don't know, Harry. I think it's just that I feel more secure doing landscapes and portraits. I tried cubes and triangles once but I got tired of them." In her mind, abstract forms were intimately associated with machines, with computers, with apartment complexes and other elements of modern life that she felt were dehumanizing. Portraiture was a celebration of the individual and landscapes celebrated nature.

Howard looked at his wife, thinking what a lovely person, what a pretty girl, what a marvelously slim neck, what pensive wisdom, what a nice couple. How pleasant it was in Connecticut, and how nicely he had worked things out for himself.

Yet something was bothering him, and had been ever since the night with June in the bar, the night she told him he was a liar and gave him the article to read.

He decided it was time to do something about June—even though he well knew she wasn't the real problem.

Next morning he walked into the office and found, thumb-tacked to his wall, a large chart fashioned from a sheet of yellow cardboard.

"Hey, June! What the hell is all this?"

June came in smiling. "That's for gold stars," she said. "Every time you tell the truth you get a gold star, okay? See?" She showed him a small box of gold stars.

Howard stared at her.

"It's not my idea," she said. "I really can't take credit for it."

Dropping into his chair, Howard jerked his necktie loose. "Well then—whose idea *is* it? Who *can* take credit for it?"

"This guy Kevin—in our Group. We were talking about the way you keep throwing paper at the trash basket, you see, and he said you obviously have a thing about games. So he thought the chart would be a good idea. We all agreed—Dr. Denison included."

Howard put his elbow on his desk and cupped his chin in his hand. "My God," he said.

"He's wonderful," June said.

"Who?"

"Kevin. He's a Broadway director. Just in his early forties. Kevin's not his real name. He had another idea. He said that when he started telling the truth he found it helpful to close his eyes." June laughed. "Hey! Look at me, Mr. Carew. Have you told any lies today?"

"No," Howard said sourly. "But the day's barely started."

June laughed again. "I'll give you a gold star for that. Just for luck." She licked one and stuck it on the chart. "I hope that's only the beginning."

Howard peeled off a Rolaid. "Of what, exactly?"

"The beginning—of a whole shower of gold stars. Good luck." She trailed from the office.

Howard chewed his Rolaid. Getting up from his desk, he walked over to inspect the chart. It was ruled in ink, as meticulously done as a piece of printed graph paper. Days of the month ran horizontally across the top, covering the remaining two weeks of August and half of September. Beneath each date there were twenty squares, meaning that on any given day he could get as many as twenty gold stars, in itself an idea that was preposterous.

In a few minutes he stood in her doorway. "June," he said. "I think you and I had better have a little talk."

She looked up from her dictionary. "Okay. When? Right now?"

He nodded. "Yeah. Right now. There are certain implications about all this that disturb me. Now. In the first place, who says I'm such a big liar that I need a gold star truth chart?"

"We all do," June said.

"*Who* all do?"

"Our Group. And Dr. Denison. Also Hank."

"The guy you live with? You mean you and Hank talk about it in bed at night?"

"Well . . ."

"You *do?*"

"Last night we did." Her eyes were innocent. "But mostly it's the Group."

"My God."

"What's wrong? Look, Mr. Carew, I still don't think you understand about Groups. There's nothing we don't talk about. Last night we talked about Dr. Denison's jockey shorts —when we weren't talking about you. They all agree with me. Would you like some coffee?"

"Agree with you about what?"

"Agree that I'm taking the right course of action. They think I'd be finking out otherwise."

"What course of action is it that you're taking?"

"The way I've decided to relate to you."

Howard took a deep breath.

"We came to agreement on three points," June said. "First, that I'm absolutely right in refusing to work for a dishonest person. Second, that if I quit I should say truthfully why I quit, and third, that I should give you a chance to reform—that I should really do my very best to try and help you find your identity. We all agreed—Dr. Denison included."

"Look, June," he said in a curt voice, "if I needed a psychiatrist I'd pay for one."

Howard returned to his office to marshal his resources. He looked at his fingernails to see if they might need clipping. They didn't. He opened the morning mail and stared long and hard at an advertisement for a sauna bath and another for a set of socket wrenches.

If it took sternness, then he had no choice but to be stern. He got up and stood in her doorway again. "The thing is, June—you're my secretary. But that doesn't give you the right to tell me how to run my personal life and particularly how to conduct my marriage."

"Quite true, Mr. Carew. I agree perfectly."

"I thought you would."

"It's exactly what Kevin said. But—the one right that I *do* have is to quit—"

"True."

"And to say truthfully *why* I quit."

Howard shook his head.

"Why are you shaking your head?"

"I'm sorry, June, I just can't take it seriously. For me to *think*—that you'd actually march up to Personnel and quit—and tell them you were quitting because I fell short of your standards on truth and honesty . . ." Howard spread his hands. "It's just something I can't take seriously."

"You should," she said. "Because if that's what it comes to, then that's what I'll do. But I hope it doesn't come to that. Please don't let it."

She opened her dictionary and then closed it over her hand. "What I really want to do is help you. Not punish you. Do you fantasize a lot?"

"Do I *what?*"

"I'm sure you must. We were talking about that last week. All inveterate liars do a lot of fantasizing. Kevin was a pathological liar when he was in his teens. He said he had himself absolutely convinced he was Joe DiMaggio. When he wasn't hitting home runs, he was in bed with Marilyn Monroe."

A man given to very light lunches, Howard found himself that day having a very large lunch at a Mexican restaurant, sitting moodily in a dark corner and gorging himself. It made him very sleepy and his eyelids felt heavy even before he got up from the table.

Two o'clock found him groggily and dyspeptically making his way along Madison Avenue, headed back to the office. At an intersection, as he stepped down from the curb, he twisted his ankle. For a few minutes the pain was intense. It woke him up in a hurry. He started cursing June.

Still cursing her, he hobbled back to the office, rode up in the elevator, limped down the hall and came to a stop in her doorway. "Any calls?"

"No calls."

He had been determined to conceal the injury from her but as he turned away he felt a stab of pain so incisive that he groaned and muttered, "Ouch!"

"What's wrong?" she asked.

"Nothing."

"Mr. Carew! You're limping!"

"A lot of people limp."

Howard sank into his chair. She followed him, looking concerned. "What happened?" Grudgingly he told her. She seemed skeptical. "Don't you believe me?" he demanded. "You think I did it jumping out of somebody's bedroom window?"

"I believe you. I mean, I believe you twisted it stepping down from the curb, yes."

Howard frowned. "Well then, what *don't* you believe?"

"You should realize it was not truly an accident. It's true," she went on, watching his face. "I'm sorry—Dr. Denison assures me there's no such thing as an accident. You twisted your ankle because things are going poorly for you and you pity yourself. You twisted it because you *wanted* to twist it. Subconsciously, you see, you willed it to happen. You have problems that you don't really want to face and subconsciously you decided that if you twisted your ankle you wouldn't have to face them. Come on, Mr. Carew—face up!"

"June . . ."

"Yes?"

He looked deep into her eyes. "Nothing."

Badly needing to blot June from his mind, Howard faced up by calling Sadie but her apartment didn't answer and when he called Barney's he learned that her mother was ill and that she had gone home to Virginia, perhaps for as long as a week.

In her absence he made a call to her immediate predecessor, one Eleanor Abernathy, a right-wing bon bon, a leggy confection with a curtain of beige hair and an unreasoning love of things French, perhaps because she had been born in Eau Prairie, Wisconsin, and numbered French furtrappers among her ancestors.

Eleanor had come to New York straight from college,

staked to a fancy East Side apartment by her wealthy parents. In two years she had not had a job of any kind. Spiro Agnew was her hero. She lived in dread of being carted away in a tumbrel.

In the old days, just before he stopped seeing her, Eleanor had taken to apostrophizing him post-coitally. It was one of the things that had driven him away. She had not changed.

"Quel homme!" she said.

"Mmmmm," Howard said, balancing an ashtray on his bare chest.

"Quel cop-u-lay-she-*on!*"

Howard's answering chuckle was forced. He gritted his teeth.

"Oh, Howard, I've missed you so, I really have. Très désolée."

"Mmmmmm," Howard replied. "Je suis fatigué." He yawned. "Je suis *pleasantly* fatigué."

The evening with Eleanor was no help at all. Worse, it made him start thinking about Norman S., the busy-bee salesman described in June's article.

Howard paused to regroup. It took him a couple of days. On the third day he called June into his office when she returned from lunch. She wore a new outfit—not so much a pants suit as a set of coveralls, black with white piping. To Howard, it was an outfit that seemed ideally suited for refueling an airplane.

As usual she perched herself on his desk. "Yes?" She started swinging her leg, waiting. Howard got up and stood by the window. "Something is happening to me, June," he said in a faraway voice.

"Is it good or bad?"

"I don't know . . ." He sighed. "I just don't know . . ." For a few minutes longer he gazed from the window, then turned. "It has to do with you, and it's something that's not really familiar to me. It's not so much a physical thing as a—hell, I don't know, sort of an all-en*compass*ing thing."

June was still swinging her leg, watching him closely. Howard shrugged and sat next to her on the edge of the desk. "I should disregard it," he said. "Because, after all, things being what they are, I have no choice. And yet . . ." He let his voice fade and looked down at the listless droop of her bellbottoms. He spread his hands and smiled, then placed his arm about her shoulder. He began patting her. "Gosh," he said in a tone of melancholy. "I don't know, I just don't know, but . . ." He looked into her eyes and said, "The trouble is, I think you're a pretty terrific girl, June . . . ever since that night in the bar . . . something has . . ." He touched her shoulder lightly, barely making contact, moving his hand like a wand to waft her body close—and then found that he was tugging instead of wafting, and June remained where she was, unyielding, solid as a rock. "Hey, cut it out!" she said.

Howard tried to laugh. He was up from the desk, feeling hot in the scalp, groping for his cigarettes.

"Look me in the eye, Mr. Carew. Look me in the eye." June's mouth began to twitch. Then she burst out laughing. "That was so pathetic I can't stand it. That look you gave me, that husky voice. Oh, Mr. Carew, you're really indescribable. You're so *totally* horrible, you're almost pure."

Howard had the tip of his cigarette between his teeth. "Okay, June, if that's the way you feel about it. If you can't recognize a perfectly honest expression of emotion—"

"Stop it, Mr. Carew! Please!" June bent double, laughing. "I just had my lunch."

"Naturally I don't expect you to reciprocate." Howard now was straining for pathos. "After all—the age differential . . ."

"That's unimportant. It's just that you don't appeal to me, you don't turn me on. I'm sorry but that's the way it is, and we both should face it."

Still perched on his desk, she began swinging her legs, looking down at her feet with a faint smile. "Do that again for me, Mr. Carew . . ."

"Do what?"

"That husky voice, those hooded eyelids. Say 'I think you're a pretty terrific girl, June.' In that husky voice." She smiled, but then the smile faded, and her eyes became grave. "It's all from fear, you know."

"What's all from fear?"

"Isn't it true? Don't we lie out of fear? No matter how much we rationalize, it always gets back to fear."

Howard looked at the hollows under her eyes.

"We lie socially," she said, "because we want people to like us. We lie to escape punishment. We lie because we're afraid that if we tell the truth, something will hurt us. And if a person is a very *big* liar, it means he's a very frightened man." With a look of sympathetic concern, June walked slowly out.

The little bitch was ruining his life, and he still wasn't sure why. All he knew was that he was using up Rolaids at the rate of a pack a day.

His poise continued to drain away. There were tell-tale signs, the most notable being an impulse he felt early one morning to do as she said and start telling the truth. He was shaving. He looked at himself in the mirror with a stricken expression. It was absolutely out of the question.

He became excitable. Both at home and at the office he displayed a sort of loud, braying joviality, puzzling both June and Charlotte. Superficially he seemed in the highest of spirits, but just as suddenly as the braying had begun it lapsed into quiet brooding melancholy.

He began to do things that struck even himself as strange. These too were tell-tale signs, small things but significant. June was upsetting the delicate equilibrium, the careful codification, that he had taken years to work out.

One evening he brought home a new suit for which he had paid $149.50. "Beautiful," Charlotte said. "How much was it?"

"It was only one-nineteen-fifty," Howard found himself saying. It was a ridiculous lie, totally alien to his code, an indication of crack-up.

Next morning Charlotte asked him what train he planned to take. He was bent upon the 7:56 but, hearing her abrupt question, his brain flashed a warning signal, bidding him reply anything at all—anything but the 7:56.

"The eight fourteen," he said, and then: "I mean the seven fifty-six. My God!"

On Friday afternoon of that week, June came into his office and said, "I'm sorry, Mr. Carew, but I've decided there's no use. It's hopeless. I'm afraid you're totally unregenerate. On Monday morning I'm going up to Personnel and give notice."

Stunned, Howard took out his nail clipper. Trying to strike an attitude of indifference, he gave her a sardonic smile and said, "You can't do that, June."

"Why can't I?"

"You haven't cleared it with your Group."

"Everything is a joke with you, isn't it?"

Howard shrugged. "*I've* got an idea."

"What is it?"

"You stay—*I'll* quit."

"Ha ha," June said with bitterness. She looked deep into his eyes, and then deep into the eyes of Charlotte, whose photograph stood in an easel frame on Howard's desk. She picked it up and looked at it closely. Then, shaking her head, she replaced it. "I feel sorry for her," she said. "She looks like such a wonderfully sensitive human being. Well . . . anyway, that's my decision."

Howard nodded. "I'm sorry to hear it, June. I'll miss you. But if that's your decision . . ." He spread his hands.

"Good night, Mr. Carew."

"Good night, June."

"Have a nice weekend . . ." She smiled back at him over her shoulder.

On Sunday morning, Howard and Charlotte were invited to brunch. When it was time to leave, Howard was still in his bathrobe, slumped in a chair on his terrace. Charlotte was dressed in bright yellow, ready to go. "I'm going on ahead," she said. "Don't forget to bring your bathing trunks."

Howard nodded and then raised his head.

"What's wrong?" she asked.

"Nothing."

After she left, Howard went upstairs and put on a record, the "Washington Post March," turning the volume high and marching back and forth along the upstairs hall, in and out of the bedroom and all around until the record ended. Then he knelt by his bed and let his head rest on the bedspread, staying there so long that when he got up and looked in the mirror there was a mark on his forehead, a bunch of grapes. He rubbed his forehead gently.

At supper that evening, Charlotte abruptly put down her fork and said, "Howard, what's wrong?"

"Nothing. Why?"

"You've been following me around all day doing that."

"Doing what?"

"Staring at me in that strange way—and then closing your eyes. What's wrong? Do your eyes hurt?"

"Nope." Howard was on his feet, heading from the room.

"Where are you going?"

"Out for a walk," he called back.

He walked through the neighborhood, moving at a slow, brooding pace, uphill and down, thinking about himself and of the turn his life had taken. There were no sidewalks and, as he had learned in the Boy Scouts, he walked to the left facing traffic. Each time a car approached, blinding him with its headlights, he stepped off to the shoulder of the road and waited for it to pass.

At first merely morose, his mood changed to one of irritation. In the roadway lay a fallen branch. Angrily he kicked at it, intending to send it flying, hoping to hear twigs snap. Instead, in the dark, he missed it completely, which gave him a very unpleasant feeling about the kneecap to go with the unpleasant feeling in what passed for his soul. Up a long slope he climbed, limping a little, and then, with even greater anger and much greater accuracy, he kicked a galvanized garbage can which stood at the side of the road. So well aimed was the kick, so solid its delivery, that the can fell over, lost its lid and went rolling down the slope with a great clatter, spilling contents as it rolled.

At that point it seemed to Howard that nothing in his life went right any more. "Dirty son of a bitch!" he snarled, and was off in hot pursuit.

Arresting the can's flight, he carried it, now less than half full, back up to its original station at the crest of the hill. He then retraced his steps, stooping to retrieve odd bits of discarded personality—a milk carton, a thick chunk of wet newspapers, an empty bottle and a surprisingly heavy coffee can

which was filled, to judge by the feel and smell, with con-
gealed cooking grease. Cradling these items in his arms, he
pressed on down the slope, picking up speed to overtake
several swatches of used facial tissue which fluttered just out
of reach in the mild breeze.

Back up the hill he trudged, on the way dropping the can
of grease and permitting a few pieces of facial tissue to slip
away. It was then that he heard a crackling male voice
shout: "Hey, what's going on out there?"

Howard stood stockstill, feeling a strong impulse to drop
everything and run.

"Who's out there? Let that damn garbage can alone, you
little bastards!"

The aroused homeowner could be heard now sprinting
over gravel—and then with a cry of great pain he was filling
the night with blasphemy.

"Elliott! What's wrong? What happened?" This was a
woman's voice, a hoarse bellow, remarkable for its power,
coming from the direction of the dimly lit house. "Are you
all right, hon?"

"Herbie—if that little bastard leaves his express wagon in
the driveway . . . one more time . . . so help me God . . .
I'll kill the little bastard!"

Howard was still on the scene, trying as best he could to
jam refuse back into the garbage can. The job was far from
complete. In addition to the coffee can of grease which he
had dropped, there were other items all over the ground, particularly at the crest of the hill, where the can had first fallen
and where the spillage was greatest. Flight now was out of the
question, for the injured party was already upon him and now
saying: "Hey! Did those dirty little bastards knock over that
can again?"

A cover-up was being freely offered. Howard grabbed it.

In the act of picking up orange rinds, he straightened with a sense of relief. "I suppose they must have . . . what dirty little bastards are you speaking of?"

"Dirty little vandalistic neighborhood bastards around here. Four times now they've knocked over our can and spilled garbage all over the road, then they run away; I'd like to kill 'em."

Howard nodded. "Kids'll do anything these days," he said. "Little bastards."

"I was just trying to clean up the worst of it for you," Howard said.

"No reason why you should. Come on, I'll get it."

"No, here, let me help . . . I'm Howard Carew, from down the road."

"Elliott Case. Every time they knock it over it takes me at least half an hour to clean it up again." Turning toward the house, Case shouted, "*What?*"

"I said you're not to call my son a little bastard, do you understand what I'm saying, Elliott?"

"Go to hell," Case muttered.

"You trying to win the Stepfather of the Month award? Is that what you're trying to do?"

"Right," Case muttered.

"I won't have you calling everything and everybody a bastard. Is that your answer to life?"

Howard found the woman's voice truly amazing. He listened with awe as it rolled through the hills.

"Okay, Regina," Case was muttering. "I guess you know what you can do, don't you?"

Howard chuckled. "Are you new around here by any chance?" he asked ingratiatingly. Case sounded like a good guy.

"Yeah, we've only been here a couple of weeks."

"I thought so," Howard said. "You see, the thing is you
don't have to bring the cans out to the side of the road. How's
your leg?"

"Better, thanks . . . You don't?"

"Good. No. The collection men go right in your yard and
take care of it."

Case was temporarily distracted. "Son of a bitch!" He had
picked up something from the ground and was inspecting it
as best he could in the faint light. "Damn if she didn't throw
away my best pipe from Germany." Addressing Howard
again, he said, "They do? Well, over in Jersey—"

"Maybe that was the whole trouble," Howard said. "A
can by the side of the road is an obvious temptation to kids."

"Where we lived before, over in Jersey, they make you
haul the cans out to the side of the road."

"Not here," Howard said.

"I'm glad you told me." Case was blowing through his pipe,
then wiping the stem hard with his sleeve. "Okay, many
thanks. Don't bother about the rest of it. I'll clean it up. My
kid brother brought me this pipe from Germany." Case knelt
next to the garbage can, in search of other treasures.

"That's very nice," Howard said. "No. Let me help you."

"Why should you?"

For a few moments, Howard didn't reply. He stood there
in silence, watching Case scrabble about in the dirt on his
hands and knees. "Well—whatever you say . . ." He turned
away.

"I wonder what else that bitch threw away," Case said.
"Okay, uh—good night, thanks again."

After a few steps, Howard turned back and for a while
longer he simply stood there. Something strange was happening to him. "Mr. Case . . ."

Case was still down on his hands and knees, pawing in the
garbage. "Yeah?"

66

"There's something I think I should tell you."

"What?"

"Well . . ." Howard looked down at the dim figure of Case and then up at the star-spangled sky. "It wasn't any bunch of kids at all," he said quite clearly. "I kicked over you can and I apologize."

Howard waited. Nothing happened.

Laughing like a hyena, he dropped to his hands and knees, next to Case. "All of which is a very good reason why I should be helping you to clean up this mess. Because I'm the one who made it."

Case seemed not to have heard, although he had stopped pawing the ground.

Still tingling, Howard groped and came up with a handful of egg shells. "Mr. Case . . . I say that I'm the one who kicked over your garbage can. I have to admit it."

"Yeah, I heard you." Case sounded dazed. "Why *did* you?"

"Actually I didn't mean to kick it over," Howard said, tossing the egg shells at the garbage can and missing. "I just meant to kick it, but not to kick it *over*, if you see the distinction." With a chuckle of self-deprecation, he retrieved the egg shells and dropped them into the can.

"Why did you want to kick it at all?" Case was moving his flattened palm over the ground in a series of widening semicircles.

"Well . . . I hardly blame you for asking that question." For Elliott Case, Howard was feeling warm affection. "You see, I was out taking a walk and I kicked at this tree branch that was lying in the road, and I missed it. Completely. That made my kneecap hurt—has that ever happened to you?"

"Not that I can remember."

"Well frankly it's like kicking air." Howard paused. "It made me mad as hell, so I took it out on the garbage can. I gave it a kick and it fell over. That's exactly how it happened.

67

So then I got to work and started picking up the stuff for you."

"That's weird," Case said. "But—no harm done, I suppose. If you hadn't done it, I'd never have found my pipe, that's one way to look at it."

"I must say you're taking a very decent attitude about it," Howard said.

Still on his hands and knees, Case swiveled his head. "*What?*"

"Where are you?" The woman was approaching, crunching over the gravel of the driveway. She stopped short. "Who's there with you?" she asked in a voice that might easily have carried to the railway depot.

"The man who kicked over our garbage can," Case said. "What in the hell did you throw away my best pipe from Germany for?"

"Who did *what?*"

She moved closer. Although the light was dim, Howard saw that her bulk matched her voice, which she made no attempt to lower even though she was now at close range.

Howard spoke up. "Mrs. Case? I'm Howard Carew from down the road. Yes, I'm the culprit, and I apologize. I was just telling your husband how it happened." Howard took a step backward. "Well, I guess the mess is about cleaned up now, so I'll be running along. It certainly was nice meeting you both," he added in a ringing voice.

"Sirrrr . . ."

Howard turned.

"Just a minute, sir . . ." Mrs. Case was pointing to the coffee can of grease which Howard was holding. "Is that ours?"

"Yes," Howard said, "At least I suppose it is. It fell out of the can."

"What are you planning to do with it?"

"Well . . ." Howard sniffed. The smell of alcohol was loud on the night air and he now judged that during the course of the evening the Cases had been doing some husband and wife drinking. "I just thought I'd get rid of it for you—since the whole thing was my fault."

"Put it back in the can."

"It won't fit," Howard said. "There's no room for it. The can's too full. I was planning to take it home and put it in my trash can for you."

"There was plenty of room for it before. Just drop it right in the can."

"There'd have been even more room if you hadn't thrown away my best pipe," Case said.

"As a matter of fact," Howard said, "the lid wasn't on tight. It was just sort of balanced on top. If the lid had been tight, nothing would have spilled—as long as we're all being honest about it."

"Being honest about what?" Mrs. Case asked.

"He kicked at a tree branch and hurt his kneecap, so then he got mad and kicked over our garbage can," Case said.

"My God!" Mrs. Case put her hands on her hips. "I'll take Jersey!"

"I realize it sounds silly," Howard said, "but—"

"Gimme Jersey!"

"—that's exactly the way it happened. I had the option of admitting it and helping you clean up the mess—or just sneaking off into the night."

Mrs. Case's mind already was on something else. Arms folded, she confronted Howard but addressed her husband. "You mean it never was any kids—in the first place?"

Case began to snicker. Getting to his feet he spoke in the tone of a man recalling something he had overlooked. It was a point he could not resist making even though it allied him with his wife. "Well now, as a matter of fact," he said, "speaking of being honest about things . . . when I first came running out here . . . he seemed perfectly willing to let me believe—"

Howard thrust the coffee can upon Mrs. Case. "Here is your grease, Mrs. Case," he said quickly. "I'll say good night now."

As he turned away, Case was still snickering. He hurried down the slope, picking up speed. He heard Case saying something to his wife and then laughing. Then he heard the mighty voice of Mrs. Case. "You're kidding!" she thundered. "My God! A grown man!"

Reaching the tree branch, Howard kicked it hard and clean, and sent it flying into a ditch.

✳ six

The thought of running to June, telling her all about it, asking her to spare his hide—all this Howard found repugnant.

Furthermore, it wasn't all that important.

The next morning he boarded the commuter train at 6:40, unprecedentedly early for him, and when he reached the office it was barely 8:30. June was not due until 9:00, and he sat at his desk, listening for the sound of her footsteps until it occurred to him that instead of coming first to her office she might go directly upstairs to Personnel.

Up like a shot, Howard strode to the elevator, rode down to the lobby, went through the revolving doors, and took his stand outside the building, scanning the crowds and wondering if she might have ridden the elevator up while he was riding it down.

And then he spotted her half a block away, standing at the curb, June in her grease-monkey suit and huge dark glasses, and with her a heavily bearded young man, Hank perhaps, dressed all in forest green.

As Howard watched, the young man bent to kiss June on the cheek and turned away. There was a knapsack on his narrow back and a camera slung about his neck. His tawny hair fell to his shoulders. To Howard he looked not unlike a hermit about to strike out for the desert. Instead, waving goodbye to June, he ran with long stiff strides for the Madison Avenue bus, calling in an excited voice to the driver as he ran.

June came on and Howard moved out to meet her. At the sight of him she stopped short and her brow creased above the dark glasses. Howard grinned. "I did something last night you might be interested in," he said. "Let's go upstairs to the cafeteria and I'll buy you a cup of coffee—was that Hank?"

"Yes," she said. "That was Hank."

He waited until they had their coffee and were seated at a small table which he had picked for the grandeur of its view. The cafeteria was on the fifty-second floor and in a slot between two buildings he could see westward all the way to the river and to the Jersey shore beyond. As he recounted the events of the night before, June's face lit up. She kept saying, "Mr. Carew!" and "Oh! Mr. *Carew!*" Her black coverall suit zipped to the throat, and her fingers were caressing the zipper, zipping it down an inch or so and then back up. Once she reached across the table and pressed his hand.

Howard kept chuckling at her reaction, telling her modestly that what he had done wasn't really all that much, but her enthusiasm was unbridled. When he had finished, she seemed ecstatic. She was oscillating. "Mr. Carew, I just can't tell you how thrilled I am—and how thrilled *you* should be."

Howard grinned. "Sure you wouldn't like to change your mind—and stop by Personnel on the way down?"

"Absolutely not!"

"Would you really have gone through with it, June?"

She took off her dark glasses and looked at him wide-eyed. "Of course. But now I'm truly glad I don't have to. Besides— I don't really think you did it because you were afraid I'd tell on you. You did it for some other reason."

"You may be right," Howard said.

When they reached the office, she licked a gold star and stuck it carefully on the chart. On the star, in tiny lettering, she pencilled G. C., and then stood back. Howard looked puzzled. "Garbage can," she explained.

"Oh, of course," Howard said.

"Just wait until I tell the Group tomorrow night! Oh, Mr. Carew, this is such an enormous breakthrough. Believe me. Just wait, you'll see. A whole new world will open for you now, and you'll be so glad. *The truth shall set you free!*"

Howard replied with a modest chuckle.

"The truth can be so *cleansing*. You'll feel so good you won't believe it. You won't even recognize yourself. And once you really start telling it, you'll find that you won't be able to get along without it. You won't be able to stop."

By the time he left the office that evening, Howard had re-evaluated the importance of the night before. There was something infectious about June's enthusiasm. Although he still had many reservations of various sorts, he began to ask if he had not been unduly harsh upon himself in so minimizing his feat. For one hitherto so poor in treasures of the spirit, it could not be regarded as totally insignificant.

Late that evening, after Charlotte went upstairs to read, he took another walk. Although he was not aware of it when he left the house, he soon realized that he was bound for the home of Elliott and Regina Case, bent upon returning to the scene.

All was quiet in the Case household. One dim light burned. A warm breeze stirred the trees, touched Howard's temples, played lovingly at his eyelids. The garbage can had stood just about here . . . and he had kicked it . . . like that . . . and sent it rolling . . . garbage spilling . . .

Howard took a deep breath, looked up at the sky and grinned. He had been standing about here, and Case had been down on his hands and knees, just about there. He had been content to let the lie pass and then—bang-o! *Mr. Case,* he had said, *there's something I think I should tell you.* Howard nodded.

It would have been an easy matter to let Case go on thinking the can had been knocked over by kids, or possibly by a raccoon.

Turning away, he walked on through the night, walked on light feet.

As he prepared for bed, he seemed to move from bathroom to bedroom with the great loping weightless strides taken by the astronauts on the face of the moon.

Charlotte was already asleep. As he loped by and lowered his weightless body to his side of the mattress, he sighed and the sigh became a shiver.

With a silly smile on his face, he lay in the dark, too excited for sleep.

The world, he told himself, shall know me in all my horror, shall know my spirit in all its bleakness. So shall I be shriven, bleached clean, a man humbled, serene in his humility, pretending nothing. Mine shall be a policy of excruciating honesty—and wherever it may lead me, so be it.

73

Although revilements may rain down upon me, yet I shall stand all unflinching, eyes shining, brow serene, Howard Carew, man of truth, a man people would find it impossible not to admire.

When he got home the next evening, Charlotte was setting the table. He kissed her and stood back, looking at her with deep contemplation. "What is it?" she asked.

"You look nice tonight." He went on into the kitchen and mixed himself a martini and then, sipping it, he stood at the sink and looked through the window. It had been raining all day and the lawn looked startlingly green in the early twilight. He noticed how precisely etched were the boundaries of Charlotte's flower beds. Something had changed. He was seeing things in clean lines. For so long he had seen the world as a smudged finger painting. Now it was a steel engraving.

Carrying the martini with him, he went upstairs to change his clothes. In the bedroom he remarked the clean lines of the white bedspread, the taut way it hugged the bed. Looking from the window, he noted the silhouettes made in the fading light by the cedars in the meadow, and by the houses scattered beyond. It was as though he were seeing it again for the first time in many years. He looked into the mirror that hung above his dresser. "My God—I'm not really very good looking after all," he muttered. It was a truth he didn't care to recognize and he spent a few minutes telling himself he was probably mistaken.

"Howard . . ."

Charlotte was calling him for dinner, and when he went down he found her in the dining room, sitting with a faroff expression in the light of the candles. Charlotte had certain days, certain moods, when she seemed to be living in a dream, when her blue eyes seemed to be swimming like a couple of bemused fish.

Charlotte's eyes stopped swimming. She picked up her fork. "Marcia called."

Marcia was the wife of his brother Fred, his only sibling and the bright jewel in a family crown notably short of gems. "What did *she* want?" Howard asked.

"I'm afraid it's another command performance."

"Oh, God," Howard said.

"Fred has landed the Ezio Pinza part . . . in a performance of *South Pacific* . . . that is being staged in Madison, New Jersey . . . by the Chickasaw Community Players . . ."

"Oh, God," Howard said again.

Howard's mother had felt that Fred missed his calling, that he should have been a musical comedy star, although she was always quick to add that this did not mean Fred was not a perfectly marvelous lawyer.

To their mother, Fred had always been FRED, whereas Howard had a sort of double name. He was always Poor Howard.

When their mother was alive, the family always dropped whatever it was doing and turned out in a body whenever Fred landed a musical comedy part, however small. It was a tradition that Fred was determined to carry on.

"When?" Howard asked.

"Opening night is August twenty-eighth."

"I'm not going," Howard said.

"You're . . ." Charlotte's fork came to rest in her plate. ". . . *what?*"

"I'm serious."

Charlotte picked up her fork again. "Something's different about you, Howard. What is it?"

"Nothing," he said. "It's just that I'm tired of all this dishonesty."

"What dishonesty?"

"The dishonesty that surrounds us—everywhere we turn,

every breath we breathe." Howard was sounding self-important. "I've finally had enough of it. So it's as simple as that.
And by the way . . ." He gestured with his salad fork.
"There's plenty that you and I should talk about, for that
matter."

Charlotte frowned. Briefly her eyes seemed to swim again.
She got up and removed the avocado plates. "That sounds so
ominous," she called from the kitchen. "Do you mean it to
be?"

"Not at all."

She returned with lamb chops and peas and they began
eating. She wasn't pressing him, he noticed; she was merely
waiting. Howard chewed his lamb chop. Putting it down, he
licked his fingers, then wiped them on his paper napkin. He
knew that all he had to do was say it quicky: *Charlotte, I'm
having an affair.* And the rest would follow.

That was the part that worried him—the rest that would
follow. Picking up his lamb chop bone, he gnawed intently.
Charlotte picked at her own lamb chop bone, saying nothing.

"Did it rain a lot out here?" Howard asked.

"Quite a bit, yes . . . Did it in the city?"

"Not too much."

Howard kept working on his lamb chop bone. When it
was clean, he put it down and wiped his fingers again. Inclin-
ing his head upward, he closed his eyes briefly. Nothing happened.

"I'm worried about the way you keep closing your eyes,
Howard," Charlotte said. "How long has it been since you
had them checked?"

"Couple of years, I guess. They're okay."

Charlotte sipped some water and then held her glass high,
looking at him through the water in the fat globular part of
the glass. He saw her eyes through the water, swimming.

"What are you doing that for?" he asked. "Looking at me through your glass . . ."

"No reason that I can think of," she said, putting the glass down.

"I know what—let's sit out on the terrace," Howard said. "Let's have our coffee out there."

"The chairs are all wet from the rain."

"I'll dry them off."

He helped her carry the dishes from the table and then wandered into her studio, standing before the canvas she had on the easel. She was painting a woodland stream, an old bridge, dappled light and shadow, a pastoral scene of great serenity. On the rail of the bridge she had etched in the outline of a bird, its head thrown back, bill parted, a thrush perhaps, although she had not yet given it color. To look deep into the painting was to dwell for these moments in the peaceful glades of Charlotte's mind. It made him feel serene and he badly needed the serenity that only Charlotte could give him. To smash it all with the blunt edge of truth—turning away, he went out to the terrace and wiped off the chairs.

While Charlotte put the dishes into the dishwasher, he strolled out over the meadow as he often did after supper, patrolling the borders, checking the high wet grass for litter. Although the meadow was not his, he felt protective of it, and he liked to keep it as clean as possible. It was by now nearly dark, but as he bent to pick up a mashed beer can he noticed a beautiful tint of rose and blue, splitting the clouds just above his house, a soft remnant gleam that came and a few seconds later was gone. Seeing it brought another stab of tenderness for Charlotte, and he thought of her bending over the dishwasher, cheek flushed, a tendril of her flaxen hair trailing.

He walked back to the terrace and sat down. In a few

minutes she joined him. "What did you say to Marcia?" he asked. "Did you tell her we'd be there?"

"I said so far as I knew we would."

"Well, I'm not going. I'm serious. I'm damned sick and tired of going all the way out to New Jersey to watch Fred sing and dance. I've done it for the last time. The hell with it."

"It's your family," Charlotte said quietly.

They sat there in the dark. Howard gazed out over the meadow, a long vista terminating in a copse that was ragged and darker still than the eastern sky, which glowed with the light of Westport. Charlotte was saying little. She seemed pensive, deep in her own thoughts. Finally she stirred. "What's all this dishonesty you say we should talk about?"

"Well . . ." He sat there thinking. "It's everywhere we look," he said. "We're surrounded by it." He moved his arm through the air, groping, then pointing. "Just for example, just as a case in point—this house. We tell people we live in a converted barn. This house is no converted barn. We just say it is because we thing it sounds good. And that's pretentious."

Charlotte's hand came down on his wrist. "Oh, Howard, honestly . . ." She was laughing.

"Our dining room is all the barn there ever was, and it wasn't any barn, it was a stable and a damned small stable at that. Two stalls big enough for a couple of Shetland ponies at best. That's what we built the house around, if you'd like to know the absolute truth."

"All right, Howard—"

"I realize it's a small thing," he said.

"Okay," she said lightly. "From now on I'll say we found this little Shetland pony stall and we did it over—into a house. We can say we've always found it a little crowded."

Howard's thoughts by now were elsewhere. He was admitting to himself that so far as that particular night was concerned he was not going to tell Charlotte a damned thing. He felt enormously relieved.

The telephone rang and, deeply abstracted, he made his way across the terrace and into the kitchen to answer it. It was his brother Fred.

"Hello there," Fred said in his usual hearty voice. "I guess you heard the news."

Howard focussed on Fred. "Yes, Charlotte told me," he said. "Great."

"It's good fun," Fred said. "You know the songs, of course."

"Yes," Howard said. "I know them all."

" 'Some Enchanted Evening' . . . that's my big one, of course. And then you know the others, don't you?"

"Yes," Howard said again. "I know them all."

" 'Nothing Like a Dame'—that's not mine, of course." Fred chuckled. " 'Bali Hai' . . ."

"Yep."

"And then, of course, 'I'm Gonna Wash That Man Right Out of My Hair'—not mine either." Again Fred chuckled. "Anyway, it's all set up for the night of the twenty-eighth, opening night. 'Honey Bun,' remember that one?"

"Yeah."

"We'll have some drinks afterward and maybe some of the cast can join us, okay?"

"No."

Fred paused. "What?"

"I said no, not okay. I'm sorry."

"Why not, chum?"

"Because—I don't want to," Howard said.

Fred was laughing. "You're not serious, I can tell."

"I'm serious," Howard said.

"Well why *don't* you want to come?"

"I just don't. I mean, I'd be perfectly willing to come except—that I don't want to. For one thing it's too damned much trouble."

"Well, we certainly wouldn't want to put you to any trouble," Fred said in an acid way he had.

"Listen," Howard said, "in the course of a lifetime I've seen you in one hell of a lot of things—"

"Mother—" Fred began.

"—starting with a tap-dance recital at the age of ten and going right on through *Student Prince* and on up to *Fiddler on the Roof* and *Hello Dolly*. So don't start telling me Mother wouldn't have wanted it this way. You're not going to make me feel guilty about it."

For a few long meaningful moments, Fred was silent. Then, in an entirely different tone, he said, "Well, there's no need to get offensive about it, Howard."

"I don't mean to be offensive about it, I just thought for a minute there you were going to hit me with Mother."

"Well, as far as that goes, you know yourself how much these things meant to her."

"That's true," Howard said. "But it doesn't seem to me to be very relevant any more. Look—"

"Okay—"

"It's a hell of a long way out to Madison, New Jersey, remember."

"Okay, chum, whatever you say. I couldn't care less. I have a hunch the curtain will go up just the same." Fred paused to let this sink in. "Anyway, I guess you're old enough to make your own decisions."

"I'm forty-seven," Howard said.

After hanging up, he poured himself a glass of water and stood at the sink drinking it. "Hey, Howard," he heard Charlotte call. "Was that—you?"

Howard wasn't entirely sure. He went back out to the terrace. "Did you hear it?"

"Every word. I'm dumbfounded. How did he take it?"

"He was—dumbfounded." Howard couldn't resist a chuckle.

"If I know Fred he won't let it go at that."

"I'll handle it."

"Howard . . ."

"Yes?"

"Are you still planning to sell real estate?"

"Of course. Why?"

"Well, for an honest man I can't think of a worse occupation. Except maybe selling used cars. What *is* all this honesty stuff, Howard? What's behind it? Tell me. I'd like to know."

"Just—I don't know. Self-awareness, maybe."

She seemed willing to let it go at that. For a long while they sat without talking, side by side in their patio chairs, gazing into the darkness. Once again he had the impression that her mind was far away. Finally she sighed. "Fall is almost here. I just love fall. There's something so cleansing about it. It's very—transitional."

"Yes," Howard said.

"Well . . ." Her head snapped up. "Anyway, I'll try to do my part. I won't say we live in a converted barn any more. I hate not to though. It sounds so Connecticut-ish."

"You're not the only one," he said. "I've been guilty of it too."

Charlotte laughed. "Well then, let's *both* stop. Let's make a pact. If it will save us from guilt, save us from intellectual anarchy . . ."

"I don't like it when you talk like that, Charlotte." Howard got up and walked out to the edge of the terrace. "You sound just like Cookie Allison, trying to be smart-aleck, so damned brittle and sophisticated. That's not what you represent to me."

"What do I represent to you?"

"Do you really want to know?" He was beginning to choke up over the nice thing he was about to say.

"Yes, I do."

"A woman of dignity and sincerity, with sensitive feelings . . . and a wonderful sense of artistry, and great decency. I'm quite serious."

Charlotte didn't reply. He heard her make what sounded like a small whimpering sound that came from deep in her throat.

"I'm serious," he said again.

She sighed. "Thank you, Howard. That means a lot to me. Thank you."

"And I love what you're painting. I was standing there looking at it earlier . . . and thinking . . ." Again he felt the lump in his throat and had to stop.

"Thank you. Thank you very much, Howard."

She went into the house and returned a few minutes later with a white sweater over her shoulders.

"Anything else happen today?" he asked.

"The Rinkers are getting a divorce," she said softly, and from her tone, her inflection, it was as though she were ticking them off.

"I'm not surprised," Howard said. "I was just thinking while you were gone . . ." He moved his chair closer to hers. "We've actually had a pretty good life, all things considered. Actually we get along together very well."

"Yes, very well, Howard . . ." It was almost a whisper. Reaching out in the darkness, she touched the back of his neck with her fingertips and began moving her hand up and down, up and down.

✳ seven

June stuck another gold star on the chart the next morning and pencilled in *B. F.*

"Brother Fred," she said. "I think I'll talk to the Group about your relationship with him. It might be very interesting. Is he your older brother?"

"Yes," Howard said. "Older and only."

"Did he bully you when you were growing up?"

"Sometimes." Howard's smile faded. "He used to hit me on the head."

"Why?"

"No reason. We'd be sitting at the dinner table and he'd go to the kitchen for more milk or something, and on the way he'd pass my chair and hit me on top of the head with his knuckles. Just for fun."

"He sounds like a real son of a bitch," June said.

"On the way back from the kitchen he'd do it too." Howard scratched his head. "He also put stuff in my bed. You know . . ."

"No, frankly I don't know," June said. "What do you mean?"

"I'd be still asleep in the morning—and he'd just pile stuff on top of me."

"Like what?"

"Anything. Shoes. Books. Pictures from the wall. My Boy Scout canteen."

"*Why?*"

"Because he thought it was funny."

June was standing by the window in his office, looking studious. Smiling, Howard sorted the mail. A few minutes later he looked up. She was still at the window, gazing out with a thoughtful expression. "Something that interests me . . . when you've made an attempt to tell Mrs. Carew about yourself, what happens? You close your eyes and then what happens exactly?"

"What happens? Nothing happens."

"I mean, what are your physical sensations, for example. What do you feel?"

"What I feel is, the hell with it."

June shook her head. "Mr. Carew . . . would you say you were a just man, a man who believes in justice?"

"Of course," he said.

"Okay, if you live a lie, particularly in a close relationship, what you're doing is forcing the *other* person to live a lie, isn't that true?"

"I suppose so, yes."

"And that's very high-handed, very unjust. They think they're living with one thing when actually they're living with something entirely different. It's like thinking you're living with a horse when all along you've been living with—a camel."

"Well," Howard said, "I certainly wouldn't want to think of poor Charlotte living all these years with a camel."

"From all you've told me, it's quite clear that she thinks she's been living all these years with a horse." June turned from the window. "Actually, the old joke is quite pertinent, isn't it?" She came over and sat on his desk. "Do you know what a camel is, Mr. Carew?"

"No." Howard grinned. "What-is-a-camel-June?"

"A camel is a horse that was created by a committee."

"That's pretty good," Howard said.

June wasn't smiling. "A rather pertinent analogy in your case, wouldn't you agree?"

"Mmmmmm . . ." He swiveled back in his chair and looked up at the ceiling. "Mmmmmmm," he said again.

"What are you thinking about?"

"Sometimes," he said, still looking up at the ceiling, "sometimes I feel that if I could take shelter . . . if I could stand in a closet and tell her . . . then maybe I could do it."

June slipped from his desk. "Where you tell her is unimportant, Mr. Carew. The important thing is to do it. You can shut yourself up in a bureau drawer and tell her if you want to."

The phone rang. She picked it up. "Oh, hi, Penelope. Yes, of course. Of course. Be just as hostile as you like, I don't mind. Really? Oh, good, that's just perfect. I'm so interested to know that you feel that way . . ." June paused. ". . . and that you're willing to, you know, *express* it." June was now listening intently. "Well, I really had no idea you felt so threatened by me, Penelope, but I can see how you might feel and . . . oh yes, of course it does, it interests me enormously. It really does . . . Okay, good, I'll talk to you later. Thanks so much, Penelope."

June hung up the phone.

Howard swiveled back in his chair again. "Why does Penelope feel threatened by you?"

"Because she's in love with Hank."

"Oh." Howard brought his chair forward. "Are you and Hank still living together?"

"Yes. Of course. Why?"

"Well, hell, I can see Penelope's point. I can see how she might consider you a threat."

"There's more to it than that."

"That sounds like enough for a starter."

That afternoon, June came in and talked with him again. "Mr. Carew," she said, "I didn't mean to discourage you with that stuff about the horse and camel. Actually, I think you're doing just beautifully. How did your brother take it? When you told him you weren't going?"

"He didn't like it much."

"That doesn't surprise you, does it? People hate hearing the truth if it's unpleasant, or if they're threatened by it. Please don't let that worry you. Besides, if you really become a completely honest person you'll be worth a hundred Freds. Your life will count for much more than his ever could." June smiled. "That appeals to you, doesn't it? I can tell."

"Yes, I suppose it does," Howard conceded.

"There's so much in store for you." June's eyes were shining. "It's such an enormous concept, truth is. Once you get into it, you'll see that it can involve far more than merely non-lying." She seemed enraptured. "It can become a way of life, a quest, even a crusade. To pinpoint the exact truth, to get exact shadings and nuances—there's something almost mathematical and scientific about it. Vistas open. Horizons spread. Even a trival life can have meaning and direction—I don't mean that your life is trivial . . ."

Howard had taken out his nail clippers and was looking at his nails.

"What are you thinking about?" June asked.

Howard, dressed in a leopard skin, had just won a world-wide Pinpointing the Exact Truth contest.

"Nothing," he said, still thinking about it. The defeated candidates were ranged beside him on a platform. It was a great thrill. He felt somehow more mature than he had felt as an undercover agent, as a man who had played side by side with Stan Musial in the high minor leagues, a man who once sat in on drums for Gene Krupa, a man who owned a brigantine slave ship. People went through phases.

"You know," June said, as if struck with a sudden thought, "it's just like Icarus."

Howard put away his nail clipper and frowned. "*What's* just like Icarus?"

"It really is, Mr. Carew, it just came to me. It's an Icarus thing. If a course of action is right, then it's *right*, and we must have the strength to pursue it, regardless of the consequences. Do you see what I mean? About Icarus?"

"Not exactly."

"He had wings and he had to use them. He had to fly up and up and keep going until he reached the sun. He had to pursue his destiny to its ultimate. He had a tragic flaw, of course. Wings that melted."

"My God, June."

"I'm going to tell that to the Group," she said. "You still don't see what I mean?"

"Not exactly. I started the day as a camel."

"If a course of action is right and inevitable, our personal imperfections and flaws don't make it any the less right and inevitable. Nor does the fact that other people may object along the way. Just because people hate hearing the truth does not make truth-telling wrong. Your job is to tell it. How they react is their bag."

June thrust out her hand. Howard looked at it for a second, then shook it.

"Press on, Mr. Carew," she said. "Let it all hang out."

✳ eight

Near Howard's home there was a quaint shopping center, the component stores of which seemed to open later and close earlier than any stores within his memory. When the shopping center was closed, which it usually was, Howard and Charlotte for years had been in the habit of patronizing a small grocery store half a mile or so from their home, more for its convenience than for the variety or quality of its stock.

Sundays and holidays alike this store opened at 7:00 in the morning and did not close until 11:00 at night. It was run by a lugubrious individual named Sattersbee, a wan, spiritless man who shuffled through life with all the elan of a professional mourner—indeed less, for a professional mourner was an actor, and Sattersbee, in mourning life, was putting on no act. He meant it. He was acting when he displayed the spurious good cheer that he gave his customers, but he was sour to the core and his life, Howard conceded, was enough to make him so. He was a man obsessed with weather. Weather was a dependable variable, and it was moreover a subject on which he was an authority, having once dwelt in some obscure area near the New Jersey coast where the sky and clouds were in full view and where one could even note the wind direction. The rain and sunlight fell alike on Sattersbee and Carew, and on the level of weather Sattersbee felt himself the equal and indeed the superior of the most wealthy of his patrons, the urbane, exurban gang who dwelt in handsome clapboard houses and rode off to New York to who-knew-what glamorous lives, at what fabulous salaries, they and their wives shopping with him only as a last resort and then only when they ran out of milk and cigarettes.

Among other things, Sattersbee was capable of being devious, a fact noted over the years by both Charlotte and Howard and irritating mainly to Charlotte. He was devious about items he chose not to stock, blaming supply, demand, labor unions, farmers, distributors, modern times—almost anything and anybody rather than himself for choosing not to stock them.

At 7:15 of a Wednesday morning, Howard shoved open the screen door of Sattersbee's store. He needed milk and toothpaste.

In a green chair of flexible metal sat Sattersbee, head in his hands. His hair was damp, carefully parted, and in the instant before the man moved Howard had a sharp impression of a still-life, noticing the straightness of the part in Sattersbee's hair, the parallel exactitude of the comb furrows, the slope of the shoulders in the dun-grey cardigan. Sattersbee had always struck him as a man trapped in the northland, unable to get back home.

"Mornin' . . . mornin' . . ." Sattersbee was on his feet, moving in behind the counter, taking his stance. "What can I do for you this mornin', Mr. Carew?"

"Well, a couple of tubes of Crest, please," Howard said.

"Two tubesa Crest," Sattersbee affirmed, slapping them on the counter.

"An a quart of milk . . . and that should just about do it," Howard said.

"All rightie . . ." Sattersbee said with a show of good cheer. Yet he seemed totally sour as he lumbered over to the dairy case and extracted a quart of milk, returning to place it on the counter. "Now then, Mr. Carew . . . ?"

It was then that Howard thought of Raisin Bran. "Oh," he said. "Were you ever able to get any Raisin Bran?" He turned, scanning the shelves.

"Naw sir, never was," Sattersbee said earnestly, a trifle too earnestly. "Just no call for it any more. I been after the man for a whole month now and the distributors just don't handle it any more. Just no call for it."

Howard nodded, looking into Sattersbee's pale blue eyes. "Nice weather," he said.

"Beautiful, just grand," Sattersbee agreed. "August's been just grand so far."

"Today looks like more of the same," Howard said.

"Gonna get warmer. Wind's comin' more to the suth-ard, maybe sou-west. Could bring some rain by night."

Howard nodded. It was the sort of exchange he and Sattersbee normally had. It was their common ground, and it was Sattersbee's pleasure, left over from his past, to use words like "suth-ard" which had a gruff simplicity that was missing in southward. By now Howard had his sack under his arm and now, according to their modest ritual, it was time to deliver a mild snapper, a farewell shot. These were always delivered by Howard, for one did not simply turn and walk out. One left with appropriate words floating back over the shoulder. "Well, we sure can't gripe about August" would suffice. Another, in time of ample rainfall, was, "Well, at least it's making the grass grow."

Now, however, Howard paused, mulling over what Sattersbee had said about the Raisin Bran. Only a few days earlier, Charlotte had commented bitterly on the subject. "The idea! Raisin Bran! You can get Raisin Bran anywhere!"

Howard continued to deliberate. He was almost to the front door when he turned back, feeling a premonition that he was about to let it all hang out. "Mr. Sattersbee . . . there's something I'd like to get straight with you . . ." It was spoken in a kindly tone, but Sattersbee looked at him with suspicion, his eyes already beginning to dart.

"Even though it's not really any of my business," Howard

went on. "It's about the Raisin Bran. This is something I think you should know. If your distributors are telling you what you say they're telling you, then they're giving you a run-around. You can buy the damned stuff anywhere. It's all over Westport."

Sattersbee was looking sullen.

"And when you say there's no call for it, of course, that's just not true. I mean, *we're* calling for it and have been for a long time. If there wasn't any call for it, of course, the Raisin Bran people would stop making it."

Sattersbee looked at him agape. His mouth began to work.

Howard gave him a benign smile. "Not that I blame you, please understand." He was impressed by his blend of firmness and reasonableness. "If you've got your reasons for not stocking a commodity—Raisin Bran or anything else—then I say well and good. I say okay. That's your affair, not mine . . ."

". . . just tellin' ya what the man told *me* . . ." Sattersbee was saying in a whining, petulant voice. ". . . that's all in the world I'm tellin' ya . . ."

"Please don't take what I said as criticism," Howard said, "because truthfully none was intended. I just wanted a clarification, more than anything else. Well . . . anyway . . ." Howard picked up his sack again. "I hope you have a very good day, Mr. Sattersbee." As he shoved open the screen door, he looked back and said, "Well, there's one thing certain, we sure can't gripe about August, can we?"

Sattersbee looked at him with bitterness and at 7:20 in the morning began wolfing down a chocolate bar.

After thinking it over, Howard decided that he had left some things unsaid. A few days later, on Saturday morning, he found at dawn's early light that he was out of cigarettes. In the past, being out of cigarettes at 6:30 in the morning meant a panic trip to Sattersbee's store.

Biting the bullet, he got through the half hour by throwing on some clothes, driving to Sattersbee's and sitting outside in the car until he saw the lights go on.

He walked in with shoulders squared, jaw set—and vision blurred from nicotine deficiency. Although by now he had decided in a general way what approach he would take, he felt that his remarks would be more impressive if he had a cigarette first.

Sattersbee was sitting in his green metal chair, just unfolding the morning paper. As Howard walked in, he looked up, scowled, and looked down again.

"Good morning, Mr. Sattersbee," Howard said. "I wonder if I could have a couple of packs of Tareytons, please."

Sattersbee made no move to rise. He was reading his newspaper. Howard felt a little dizzy. He was about to repeat his request when Sattersbee put down the paper, moved slowly behind the counter and produced the cigarettes, glowering all the while.

Howard clutched at a pack, ripped it open, pulled out a cigarette, lit it, and took a vast drag and then another. Backing against the canned soups, he tried to look Sattersbee in the eye, but Sattersbee would have none of it. He was looking everywhere but at Howard.

"Mr. Sattersbee," Howard said, taking another deep drag, "I'd like to have a little talk with you, open and above-board, one human being to another."

Sattersbee looked at him as if he felt he were being addressed by a lunatic.

"When I said what I said about the Raisin Bran a couple of days ago, I meant no criticism, none whatever, and I'd like you to know that."

Sattersbee placed a finger on the cash register, lips moving as if he were doing a little mental arithmetic.

"You see," Howard said with an apologetic smile, "late in

92

life I've decided that truth is a very very important commodity. There's not enough of it in the world, and all I'm trying to do is, well, you know . . . do my part to make things more truthful."

Howard turned aside, not particularly liking the way he was expressing it. "I'll also have a quart of milk," he said.

Still speaking not a word, Sattersbee lumbered back to the dairy case, deliberately taking his own sweet time about it. Finally he returned and placed the carton on the counter.

"That should do it," Howard said. "Well . . . when do you think this northeast wind is going to stop blowing?"

Sattersbee made no reply. Putting the items into a sack, he took the five dollar bill Howard offered, handed him the change and headed back for his chair and his morning paper.

"Well . . ." Howard shoved open the door, trying to think of a snappy farewell shot. "See you later," he said.

Sattersbee rustled his paper and said nothing.

When Howard got home it was still only 7:15. It was his custom to get his own breakfast on weekends so that Charlotte could sleep. After putting on a pot of coffee, he dumped some cereal into a bowl and then poured in milk from the carton he had just brought home.

He frowned.

Sticking his nose close to the open spout, he recoiled. The milk was not only sour. It was very very sour.

It smelled like milk that had come straight out of the sour-milk department.

After breakfast he left the house with the carton of sour milk under his arm and drove back to the store. He came straight to the point. "Mr. Sattersbee," he said, "this milk you sold me is sour." He placed the carton on the checkout counter. "Smell it."

Sattersbee shook his head.

"Just *smell* it," Howard said, bending to smell it himself. His nose wrinkled.

Sattersbee dropped heavily into his green chair and picked up the morning paper. Howard glared. "Mr. Sattersbee . . ."

"I don't want to smell it," Sattersbee said.

"Well then, take my word for it," Howard said. "It's plenty sour. I'd like another carton to replace it."

"No sir-ree," Sattersbee said.

"*What?*"

"No sir-ree."

"Listen, Mr. Sattersbee—what is this? You can't sell people sour milk without expecting to make good on it."

"How do I know it's sour?"

"Well here—smell it!"

Sattersbee shook his head. "I got no intention to smell it, no intention in the world."

"All right then, take my word for it. It's just as sour as hell. It's the sourest milk I ever smelled in my life. And I want you to replace it with another carton."

"No sir-ree." Sattersbee looked up briefly from his paper.

"I'm asking you to smell it," Howard said.

"I'm sayin' no," Sattersbee said.

"Well I'll be damned," Howard said.

Sattersbee looked down at his paper again. With a final glare, Howard stomped out, slamming the door behind him, leaving the sour milk on the counter. Sattersbee's mouth was working, as if he were trying to fight off a smile.

✳ nine

On Monday night, Charlotte went off to a gypsy moth meeting. Television was offering the Monday night Game of the Week, and Howard was lying downstairs on the daybed in the room he called his den, watching the New York Mets engage the Houston Astros. Between innings he did sit-ups to strengthen his stomach muscles.

When the telephone rang it was the bottom of the sixth, and Howard at the time had just gone to the kitchen to find something to eat, settling upon a can of salted peanuts. The caller was Cookie Allison, and the sound of her voice acted as a trigger. Howard felt they saw far too much of the Allisons.

Cookie considered herself personable. It showed sometimes in the way she talked on the phone. "Good evening," she said as Howard answered. "Whom do I have the honor of addressing?"

Howard grasped his upper lip with his bottom teeth. "Hi, Cookie," he said. "Why aren't you at the gypsy moth meeting?"

"Gypsy moths bore me. Does that mean Charlotte's not home?"

"She's at the gypsy moth meeting." The can of salted peanuts stood open on the countertop. Howard took a few.

"Well, listen, do you guys have the night of the twenty-seventh open? Do you have her calendar handy?"

"Yes." The calendar was thumbtacked to a bulletin board

which hung just over the can of salted peanuts into which Howard now dipped again. "It's right here."

"Good. Is that night open?"

"Yep." Howard held the can to his lips and tilted it.

"Good. Well write us down . . . What did you say, Howard?"

Howard was giving himself a moment of pause, not quite sure he was capable of going through with it. "I'm sorry, Cookie," he said. "My mouth was full of salted peanuts."

"We want you guys to come here for dinner—what did you say?"

"I'm chewing," Howard said, and coughed.

"Did you swallow a peanut the wrong way?"

"Yes, I must have."

"Have you written us down, Howard?"

Howard finished chewing. "No," he said. "I haven't."

"You mean you can't make it? You just finished telling me that night is wide open. Is it open, or isn't it? Howard, are you loaded?"

"Nope."

"Well can you make it or can't you?"

Howard was dipping into the peanuts again.

"What you mean is that you *can't* make it, is that what you mean?" Cookie pressed.

"Yes, I guess that's what I mean," Howard said. "It's not that you don't have nice food, Cookie."

"Howard, are you all right?"

"Yes, I'm fine."

"Have I done something to offend you, Howard?"

"Not at all."

"Then what are you trying to tell me?"

"Do you mind if it's the strict—truth?"

"No, go ahead, Howard, I can take it."

"Well, I think we see each other too often," Howard said after a pause.

"You *what?*"

"Look, Cookie, I've been doing some thinking lately, and I just feel our social relationship is all out of proportion to the real bond between us."

"I'm sorry, Howard. Stop chewing. What did you say?"

"I'm sorry, I know it may sound harsh. I said I feel our social relationship is out of proportion to the real bond *between* us. I think we should taper off a little—and then when we *do* see each other we'll appreciate it more. I'm not saying this out of cruelty, you understand. Only out of sincerity and honesty. Hey, Cookie, are you still there?"

Cookie had hung up.

Howard went back to the television set but found that he wasn't concentrating on the game. He didn't feel quite right about what he had done. He knew that in any event he couldn't let it rest where it was. Actually he had mixed feelings about the Allisons. He liked Harry, a big burly, jealous guy with a low hairline and small eyes that gave him a resemblance to Java Man. Harry had a cabin up in the mountains of northern Pennsylvania and a couple of times he had had Howard up to fish trout streams. And in a way he felt sorry for Cookie, because she kept craving what she didn't have and made up for it by trying to be glib and sophisticated. Now ten years deep in a second marriage, she developed a yen for almost every man she considered more polished than Harry and this included just about every man she met. Part of the reason may have been that Harry worked in Bridgeport, where he had his own scrap iron company. Cookie seemed to feel that a husband lost something by working in Bridgeport, particularly in scrap iron.

Snapping off the television set, Howard went out and trudged down the road. The Allison house, even in the dark, looked most impressive, with its brand-new paint job of mustard yellow. Harry did very well in scrap iron. The new paint glittered, catching tiny highlights from the stars.

He knocked and Cookie opened the door. "Hi, Cookie," he said. "Listen, I'd like to explain."

Cookie's hair, blonde gone grey, was tinted silver and had been for many moons. She wore a beige pants suit with a belted over-blouse. "You've already explained," she said with a harsh laugh.

"No," Howard said. "Not completely. I realize that what I said must have sounded abrupt. The fact is, I like you and I like Harry."

"That's good to hear, Howard. That's awfully good to hear."

"Can I come in?"

"Why not?" She stepped back and Howard stepped in, touching her arm compassionately as he passed. She led the way into the living room, trailing behind her an ambiance that could only be described as acrid.

"Can you accept that, Cookie?"

Cookie sat on the arm of the sofa. Her eyes looked greased, as if she had rimmed them with vaseline preparatory to going to bed. "Accept *what*, Howard?"

"The fact that I like you and Harry."

Howard sat on the other arm of the sofa. From the opposite arm, Cookie looked at him very hard from her greased eyes. "That's nice, Howard."

"You know . . ." Howard said. "Here I am sitting here on the arm of this sofa, thinking I'd like very much to have a cup of coffee, and then realizing I shouldn't ask for one because you're irritated and hurt."

"Hurt!" The word was an expletive of denial.

"And then I think to myself that if I want a cup of coffee there's no reason not to ask even though—"

"God almighty, Howard!" Cookie was leaving the room. "How do you want it?"

"Black," he called after her. "Thanks, Cookie."

Quickly she returned with a cup of black coffee, lukewarm. "You of all people," she said. "Howard Carew, the very soul of tact and politeness."

Howard smiled.

"Have you been to a guru, Howard?"

"Well, in a way, yes."

"He's done wonders for you."

Howard sipped his coffee. "It's true, Cookie, that I've had some thoughts lately about people being honest with each other, and this is the way I feel. I feel we trade dinners from boredom, that's all. To overcome boredom, we eat at one another's houses. We drink and eat and when the evening is over we go home—feeling we've accomplished something, feeling we've had a good time, when in fact all we've done is eat and drink. Now damn it, Cookie, that's just not right. We're all good enough people, not bad people certainly—but somehow we've lost our way. We've been doing something that's essentially dishonest."

Cookie nodded. "Like eating and drinking. I can see your point, Howard. I'm beginning to understand what you're driving at. And I'm beginning to feel a little dirty."

"No need for that. As I say, we're all good enough people and for that matter it's not limited to us. It's widespread. It happens to a lot of couples."

Cookie was now standing before the mantle. She hitched up the pants of her pants-suit and smoothed the blouse over her hips. For some reason Howard at that moment recalled that she had spent two weeks that spring at a beauty ranch. Abruptly he felt sorry for her. She was smiling faintly. "I had the mistaken notion that you found me attractive, Howard. That night we all got drunk and danced to those old Benny Goodman records . . . that night when you and I danced together I could *tell* you found me attractive, in fact you wanted to slip off to bed with me."

Howard nodded gravely. Frowning, he set down his cup and began to pace, stopping before the window and peering out into the night.

"What is it you're doing, Howard?"

Howard was still looking out the window. "I'm trying to get the precise nuance of my feeling," he said. "I don't want to say anything off the top of my head."

"No, for heaven's sake, don't do *that*, Howard."

"What I think is that you're right, that I—this is the total truth, Cookie—that I probably did want to go to bed with you that night, you see, yet as I think back on it . . . Well, for instance, let's take right now as a case in point."

"What *about* right now as a case in point?"

"Well, I think I'd like to go to bed with you right now, and yet I would and I wouldn't—do you have any idea what I mean?"

Cookie let go with another harsh laugh and touched the tinted tips of her hair

"I mean frankly, in my heart of hearts—"

"Let's leave your heart of hearts out of it," Cookie said.

"What I mean is that I would, because you're an attractive woman. And yet I don't truly in my heart of hearts find you all *that* attractive." Howard spread his hands, palms upward, a gesture of sincerity. "In other words the act would be disproportionate to the feeling-tone. I mean, you asked me how I feel—that's exactly how I feel."

Cookie nodded. "You've finished your coffee, Howard?"

"Yes, Cookie, I have. It was very nice."

"Well then, Howard, get out."

Howard shook his head. "I'm sorry you feel that way, damn it, Cookie. I don't want you to hold this against me. I'm only trying to be honest, what the hell."

"So am I, Howard. I really am. And I honestly want you to get the hell out."

"Okay," Howard said. "Maybe after you think it over you'll respect me more in the long run. Maybe it'll even bring us closer together, in the long run." He shrugged. "Good night, Cookie."

"Good night, Howard, you silly bastard."

As Howard closed the door behind him, a car entered the driveway. Harry Allison got out and offered Howard a greeting. "Howard? Is that Howard? Hi, Howard, howsa boy?" Harry's hand was like a slab of warm meat and his handshake was powerful. "Where's Charlotte?"

"She's at a meeting," Howard said. "I just dropped by for a few minutes and Cookie was kind enough to let me have a cup of coffee."

"Couldn't she do any better than that? Come on back in and we'll have a drink."

"No thanks," Howard said. "I don't think it would be such a good idea." He paused. "She's mad at me."

"Charlotte?"

"No. Cookie."

Howard noticed that the front door was ajar. Harry meanwhile was letting it sink in. "Why?" he asked. "Why should Cookie be mad at you?"

"Something I just told her," Howard said. "Nothing important."

It was an answer that Harry didn't seem happy with. "Well, are you gonna let me in on it or aren't you?"

"Ask Cookie," Howard said in a tone designed to pacify. "She'll tell you."

"What the hell's going on around here?" Harry muttered.

The front door swung wide. "It's nothing, Harry." Cookie stood in the light from the foyer, and her face was shining with vaseline.

"*Nothing?* What the hell's all the mystery about?"

"No mystery, it's all very simple," Cookie said. "I phoned Charlotte to ask the Carews for dinner next week. Charlotte wasn't there. Howard answered and turned me down. He didn't want any part of it. That's all."

"That's *all?*" Harry paused. "Whaddya mean he didn't want any part of it? What kind of answer is that?"

"It's a long story," Cookie said. "There was much more to it than that."

"How much more?"

"Well . . ." Cookie gave the same bitter laugh. "You certainly don't have to worry about it. Howard doesn't find me attractive enough to have an affair with, so don't worry. He just told me so very bluntly."

"Howard . . . doesn't find you attractive enough . . . to have an affair with?"

"This is getting blown all out of proportion, Harry," Howard said.

"You turn us down for dinner and then you come down here and tell my wife—" Harry broke off and put his hands on his hips. "How in the hell did the subject of having an affair come up in the first place, if you don't mind me asking?"

"It never did," Cookie said quickly.

"Now listen, baby . . ." Harry said.

"Come in the house, Harry. Good night, Howard." Cookie grabbed Harry's arm and pulled him toward the door.

"Good night," Howard said.

"Yeah, good *night*, Howard," Harry growled. "Drop around again sometime—when *I'm* home."

✳ ten

A couple of evenings later, Howard was still letting it all hang out.

That afternoon he left the office early because he and Charlotte were scheduled to play tennis next door with their friends and next door neighbors, Bob and Alicia Wickes.

If Howard had been given his choice, if he had been told that he could have one couple as close friends and one couple only, his self-interest was such that he would have chosen the Wickeses without hesitation—not for their personalities, which he found adequate, but for their tennis court. Over the years they could not have been more generous. Not only were Howard and Charlotte invited to play when the Wickeses were playing—they were also permitted to use the court on their own. Howard's only obligation was to call in advance, a mere formality, little more than a courtesy, and the court was his for the asking. When he was finished, he brushed the court and cleaned the dust from the taped white lines so that all would be ready for the next players—this was all that seemed to be expected of him and what he received in turn was enormous pleasure as well as frequent exercise. At periodic intervals, to cement an already solid relationship, he gave the Wickeses a gallon of whiskey which often lasted them as much as a full week.

Bob Wickes was in his early forties, the father of six, a Notre Dame graduate and a wealthy man, self-made and proud of it. When long hair became fashionable, Wickes had gone in for a compromise, ending up with a hairdo reminiscent of Julius Caesar's. His hair was blonde and if there was any grey it didn't show. He was a man who remained in superb physical condition, winter and summer. Having conquered the business world so quickly, and leaving the children mostly to Alicia, he seemed to find physical conditioning far more important than anything else in his life. Often in the course of a singles match, Howard stood waiting patiently while Wickes dropped his racket and put his muscular stringy body through ten or fifteen pushups, or chinned himself from a tree limb. His tennis court was beautifully kept, as was his wife Alicia, a cheerful, chunky blonde with a two-handed backhand and inexhaustible energy.

Although human beings tend mainly to like what they are good at, Howard loved tennis even though he was lousy at it. He loved the exercise, he loved being out in the air, he loved sweating—and he loved the rare occasions when he met the ball cleanly and sent it skimming low and true over the net.

That evening he hurried home from the train and got into his tennis togs. Alicia had taken all six children to the dentist, and while they waited for her to return Howard played a set of singles against Bob Wickes and was trounced, 6-2. Then he and Charlotte played doubles against Bob and Alicia, and although they lost it was more Howard's fault than Charlotte's. Howard was worse that evening than usual. Charlotte played well. She was nicely coordinated, clean-limbed, and he found himself distracted by looking at her, watching the way she moved after the ball, admiring the loose, powerful way she reached high and brought down her racket when she served. He liked the long golden flow of her legs in the abbreviated white tennis dress. Watching her that evening gave him the same clean, well-ordered sense of form and serenity that he got from looking into one of her paintings.

He wondered why she had not been painting.

He had noticed. Her woodland scene had not progressed.

The canvas was just as it had been, the outline of the bird still only sketched, without plumage, without flesh and color.

When the set ended, Alicia had to go in and fix supper for the kids. Howard and Charlotte went on home, leaving Wickes drinking a can of beer, sitting on a bench near midcourt.

When Howard reached the house, he looked again at Charlotte's canvas. "You haven't done any painting the last couple of days," he said.

"No." She sat in a rocker in the kitchen, with her racket resting on her bare knees. Her face was still flushed and her hair was damp.

"Why not?"

"I don't know." She held her racket in front of her face and looked at him through the strings. "I just haven't felt like it."

While she fixed supper, Howard went outside and was rambling thoughtfully over his meadow when he saw an object sail through the air and land perhaps twenty feet away. When he reached it he saw that it was a beer can, mashed almost flat. Muttering to himself about people who desecrated nature, he picked it up and stuffed it into his hip pocket. It had come from the direction of the tennis court, and now he could see Wickes in a gap between two sections of the high hedge which helped to screen his court. He was still in his white tennis shorts and white shirt.

Howard started walking. "Oh ho!" he called jovially. "So you're the culprit, eh?"

Briefly it occurred to him that just after using a man's tennis court might not be the best time to take him to task about beer cans, yet he felt he could do it with safety. One thing he had going for him was the easy, joshing relationship that he and Wickes had with each other, one that permitted almost any remark so long as it had the sound of levity.

Wickes had turned away but now, seeing Howard, he turned back and cocked his head to indicate that he had not heard.

"So *you're* the dirty bastard who's been throwing beer cans into the meadow . . ." Howard said, approaching with a wide grin.

As Howard drew closer, Wickes looked at him without expression.

"I've been picking these damned things up for months," Howard said in a tone of good fellowship. "I kind of had a suspicion it might be you." He laughed. "You're the only guy in the neighborhood who's strong enough to mash them flat. Why in the hell don't you cut it out, Wickes?"

Never one to waste a second so far as physical conditioning was concerned, Wickes held a tennis ball which he kept gripping, and each time he gripped it a long rope of muscle popped up along his forearm. It was now his turn to be jovial. "First you gotta show me a deed," he said. "Some proof of ownership."

"The green earth belongs to us all," Howard said with a grin. "Okay, go ahead, Wickes." He shrugged. "You keep throwing beer cans, I'll keep picking them up. I need the exercise anyway."

"You sure do," Wickes said.

"No wonder the younger generation thinks we're a bunch of litterbugs," Howard said. "A bunch of environment polluters. I'm gonna get Joan Baez on you."

Howard chuckled. Taking the flattened beer can from his hip pocket, he tossed it straight up and caught it as it came down. Then, saying, "Think fast!" he tossed it at Wickes, who made a wild stab for it with his free hand but missed. He looked annoyed as he reached over and picked it up without bending his knees.

106

"See ya, Bob." Grinning, Howard headed for home. "Thanks again for the game," he called back over his shoulder.

Wickes made no reply. He was standing in the rays of the setting sun, the beer can in one hand, the tennis ball in the other.

The commuter set was not without caste. In terms of job prestige, Howard's placed him somewhere near the middle. Among those who were several notches up on him were Wickes, with his wealth and his tennis court; and Wickes's special friend Mark Patterson, a top editor on a top national magazine. Patterson was a man of wan elegance, sardonic wit and Ivy League drawl, all in key with the square jaw and the tortoise-shell glasses that he was continually taking off and dangling by one temple-bar. Patterson seemed to find it very amusing that anyone could spend the best years of his life editing a semi-annual magazine called *The Electron*. Beyond this, he seemed to find Howard amusing on general principles. At the sight of Howard his eyes lit up. He would start grinning—often not saying anything, just grinning. There were times when Howard wanted to kill the son of a bitch.

A few mornings after the beer can episode, Howard arrived at the railway depot to find Wickes and Patterson there ahead of him, waiting on the platform for the train, both in crisp blue seersucker. At the sight of Howard, Patterson started grinning. "Good morning, Howard," he said and then waited expectantly, eyes twinkling, as if he expected Howard to do or say something for his further entertainment.

"Good morning, Mark." Howard turned to Wickes and said, "Hi, Bob, how's it going?"

"Morning, Howard," Wickes said. "Just great." Setting down his attache case, he fell face forward, breaking the fall with his outstretched palms and going into a series of lightning pushups, springing lightly to his feet as the train roared in.

Howard had been counting. "Fifteen," he said.

Wickes grinned. "Fifteen," he affirmed and followed Patterson onto the train.

Although Howard had expected nothing less, he was relieved to find Wickes just as friendly as ever. The nearest public tennis court was fifteen miles away.

Having heard the Wickeses mention that they would be away the weekend of August nineteenth, Howard now called in advance to ask permission to use the court while they were gone—a formality.

"Howard, I'm sorry, old buddy," Wickes said. "I'm afraid it has to be negative. Alicia's sister and her husband are going to be taking over the house for the weekend while we're gone, and they're having a bunch of people up with them. A real houseful. I know they'll be using the court most of the time, both days."

This seemed reasonable enough—until Howard happened to realize along about mid-afternoon of Saturday that he had heard no sound from the tennis court; nor, so far as he could tell, was there anyone in residence.

The same thing was true of Sunday.

On Tuesday morning he saw Wickes again at the depot. Wickes was standing on the platform alone, reading the *New York Times* while he waited for the train. Expecting Wickes to say something about tennis courts, or sisters or weekends, Howard greeted him heartily and was surprised when Wickes said nothing about any of the three.

Yet, as before, he was extremely cordial.

The episode passed from Howard's mind, only to return a couple of days later. On Thursday evening, home from work by 6:00, he thought it might be very nice to play a set of tennis with Charlotte. The evening was gorgeous and the prospect was for at least a full hour of daylight if they played first and ate later. He called. Alicia answered, and he asked if it would be okay to use the court. Her tone was warm and friendly but her refusal was firm and, as it turned out, evasive.

"I'm sorry, Howard," she said. "The court is very soft. Bob doesn't think anybody should use it until it hardens up again."

Howard tried to remember when it had last rained.

So confident had he been of playing that he already had on his white tennis shorts and was holding his racket. He stood at the kitchen sink, muttering.

Fifteen minutes later came the flagrancy. From the direction of the tennis court he heard voices and then the sound of racket meeting ball. He rushed out to have a look. Alicia and Bob were playing.

"Charlotte!"

"What?" Her voice came from a distance.

"Where are you?"

"Down here."

Charlotte too was dressed for tennis. When she found the court off-limits, she had gone down to the meadow and was now lying under a tree. Howard hurried down. She had a dreamy expression on her face, peering up at the branches. "Do you see what those sons of bitches are doing?" he demanded. "Look!"

"Yes," Charlotte said. "I see." With her hands behind her head, she continued to look up at the branches.

"I don't know what to do about it," Howard said.

"What *can* you do about it?" Charlotte sat up and brushed her shoulders. "It's their court."

"I know it's their court—but what in the hell are they trying to do? They're being real bastards about it!"

Howard wandered back up to the terrace and slumped into

a chair, listening to the sound of racket meeting ball. Hearing the sound of explosive laughter, he alertly rushed out far enough to get a view. Angrily he stared at the beautifully kept court where two white-clad figures were moving against the backdrop of a huge faroff willow. "Dirty sons of bitches," he muttered.

Charlotte was trailing up from the meadow. She joined him on the terrace, stretching out her legs and wriggling the toes of her white sneakers. "Have you done anything to make him mad, Howard? I know you haven't beaten him at tennis, that's for sure."

Howard told her about the beer can episode.

Charlotte smiled. She put her hand on his knee. "That's the answer then. I guess it's the public courts for us. Do you feel it was worth it?"

Howard was scowling out over the meadow. "I can't believe anybody would be that petty. By God, I'm going to have it out with him."

Charlotte had started for the kitchen. She paused and turned. "Howard . . . I don't think you should start anything. He's awfully strong, you know. He's always doing all those exercises. Alicia just bought him a rowing machine for his birthday."

"What are you suggesting?" Howard got up and followed her. "That he's going to do me physical harm? Grown men don't go around doing that sort of thing, at least not in Connecticut they don't. Besides, I'll be totally civilized about it. I always am. Hell—he's my friend!"

A couple of mornings later, Howard saw his opportunity. He followed Wickes onto the train and bided his time until Wickes took a seat next to the window. Then Howard sat down next to him, feeling immediately unwelcome.

With his *New York Times* spread wide, Wickes grunted

what might have been a greeting or might have been a pro-
test, Howard was unsure. But such was his determination that
he didn't really care. Wickes had not only been petty and
glaringly obvious, he had also been a total hypocrite, with his
friendly greetings at the depot and his friendly telephone
voice. If ever Howard felt he was justified in taking a stand,
he felt it now.

It gave him a sense of satisfaction to realize that in a way
he held Wickes captive, for it would be a truly flagrant act
for the man to get up now and change his seat. It was also
interesting to see that Wickes had given up any pretense of
cordiality.

Howard waited until the train was nearly to Norwalk.
Then he said, "Bob, there's something I'd like very much to
talk to you about."

"What's that?" Wickes murmured, eyes still on the account he was reading of dollars and yens.

"I want you to realize first of all," Howard said, "that I'm
approaching this in a spirit of reason, with no hostility whatever."

"Approaching what?" Wickes asked softly.

"What I'd like to feel," Howard said, "is that I'm not even
involved—that instead I'm somebody away up in the air,
looking down upon two people riding on a train and talking."

Wickes looked puzzled.

"That's why I'm approaching it in a spirit of objectivity,"
Howard said.

"Okay, Howard . . . approaching *what?*"

"Your tennis court and various other matters," Howard
said.

He saw Wickes stiffen, saw him reach for the forelock of
his Julius Caesar hairdo and capture a strand between his first
and second fingers.

"I think if two people can't be honest with each other, then it's a hell of a world," Howard said.

"Right, Howard, I agree," Wickes said, still twisting his hair, still reading his paper.

"The point being, of course, that it's *your* tennis court," Howard went on. "You roll it, maintain it, open it in the spring, close it in the fall. You bought and paid for it."

Wickes nodded. "Right, Howard. All those things are true."

Howard could tell that Wickes was no longer reading his paper even though he still pretended to. He also noticed a smudge of lipstick on the lapel of his seersucker jacket. "So you have a perfect right, Bob, to keep off anybody you choose to keep off."

"Okay, Howard. So what else is new?"

Howard remained silent, trying to get it all straight in his mind so that it would come out exactly as he wanted it to come out. Above all he didn't want it to sound as if he were more interested in tennis privileges than he was in the principle involved.

While Howard was getting it straight in his mind, Wickes was twisting his hair, with a strand now curled tightly over his index finger. He was also churning and chafing, Howard could tell, and was filled with hatred and doubtless even disbelief that in the sophisticated commuter world a man could be talking with such naïveté.

Howard chuckled. Wickes' lip seemed to lift. "Bob," Howard said, "what you probably can't understand is that I'm approaching this in a totally non-hostile spirit."

Wickes was approaching it in no such spirit. With great labor, he now opened his newspaper to the sports section, elbowing Howard's rib cage as he did so and not bothering to apologize.

"I'd like to think," Howard said, "that all this will somehow bring us closer together."

"What will?" Wickes was looking at a quarter-page advertisement for karate lessons.

"This little talk we're having."

"What talk?" Wickes was letting his gaze linger long upon the karate ad. His bronzed brow was creased as he seemed to concentrate upon it. One hand was again up at his forelock, the other was grasping the edge of his newspaper, very tightly. They were strong hands, without question.

"I'd personally prefer to remain friends," Howard said. "But even at the risk of jeopardizing our friendship I still have to say what's on my mind." Briefly he closed his eyes. "I'm not going to make any particular issue of your apparent compulsion to squeeze beer cans and throw them into the field. I'm not going to take any moralistic stand on that, nor even any good-citizenship stand. I occasionally litter. We've all littered at one time or another."

Wickes had finally let go of his hair. He was gazing from the window, hands folded on top of the karate ad.

"And moreover," Howard said, "I think you have a perfect right to keep certain people off your tennis court. What gets me, Bob—and what I think is clearly wrong—is to link the two. It's your business, of course, but it's also my business to speak up, and to speak the truth."

Wickes was still looking at the passing scenery. The knuckles of his right hand were taut from the grip he was putting on his kneecap, gripping and releasing, as if his kneecap were a tennis ball. His hair by now looked untidy.

"For years," Howard pressed on, "we all had a very good relationship—and then, a week or so ago, I took a critical attitude about the beer cans, even though you'll have to concede that I expressed myself in a nice way."

Wickes was looking disgusted.

"I'd simply like to ask you a simple direct question," Howard said. "Whatever your answer is going to be—I have no choice but to abide by it. The question is this—did you kick us off your tennis court because I criticized you about the beer cans?"

Still looking at the passing landscape, Wickes very much resembled a man trying to control both his emotions and his body.

"If so," Howard said, "I don't think it shows a very mature attitude toward ownership—or toward criticism."

Although he was still looking through the window, Wickes finally spoke. "Let's get one thing straight, Howard," he said in a low voice. "The reason I'm not letting you use my tennis court any more is very simple. It's because I don't like you."

"Hah!"

"Hah?" Wickes now turned, with a look of amazement. "Whaddya mean, *hah?*"

"I just know you're not serious," Howard said. "I just know—"

"Know I'm not *serious?*" Wickes shook his head. He seemed more relaxed now. He had folded the newspaper and stuffed it down next to his leg. "You mean you find it all that hard to believe that somebody doesn't like you? Do you feel you're all that likable?"

"No, that's not what I'm saying. I'm saying—"

"Hell, Howard, nobody likes *everybody*. And you're not one of the people that I happen to like. It's as simple as that."

With obvious pleasure, Wickes looked at his own hands. They were laying open on his lap, palms upward, fingers curled.

Howard shook his head. "I think you're deliberately clouding the issue, Bob. You can't just suddenly decide—"

"Suddenly *decide?* Suddenly decide, hell. There's nothing sudden about it. I've *never* liked you very much."

Howard shook his head doggedly. "I find that very hard to believe," he said.

"Well *why*, for God's sake?"

"It just doesn't coincide with the facts," Howard said. "No, Bob, obviously you're just using it as an excuse. Come on, let's be honest."

"Howard, listen, goddammit, I'm *being* honest." Wickes looked him straight in the eye. "I've never been more honest in my life. I don't like you."

Howard's face was beginning to feel very hot, and so too were the roots of his hair. "Well, then you've been one hell of a hypocrite over the years," he said.

Wickes reached beneath his seat, pulled out his attaché case, opened it and took out a sponge rubber ball, which he began squeezing. "A person needs a certain amount of hypocrisy to get by in this life," he said, sliding the attaché case beneath his seat again. "Hell, Howard, this isn't the kind of thing you go around telling people to their face. It's the kind of thing you tell your wife at night in bed. But you forced it out of me. So there it is."

"There what is?"

"The fact that I don't like you."

"Okay, Bob, at least you're being honest—assuming that you *are* being honest, that is."

"I'm being honest as hell," Wickes said.

"Okay, okay, the hell with it then." Howard tried to keep rancor out of his voice, tried to remain reasonable. "Okay, Bob, this is all perfectly reasonable, I suppose. So now you can do me a favor. You can tell me what it is you don't like about me. Go ahead. Be honest."

Wickes shook his head. "I really don't know, Howard. It's not something I can put my finger on. It's just that some people you like and some you don't like, that's about as close as I can come to it. Oh, hell, I could enumerate a lot of things, for that matter, but that wouldn't be getting at the root of it."

"What kind of things?"

"Well—you always do a lousy job of brushing the court when you're through playing. You always do it, but you always do it lousy."

Howard's mouth was grim. "Okay, go ahead."

"Well, most of the time you act silly as hell for your age. A lot of people have commented on it."

Once more Howard felt heat rush to the roots of his hair. "Who?"

"I won't mention any names."

"People in the community?"

"I said, I won't mention any names," Wickes said happily. "Another thing to consider—oh, the hell with it. I don't know how to express it any more clearly than I've already expressed it. You're just a guy I don't happen to like, that's all." Wickes studied the rubber ball. "Yes, there is one other thing that drives me crazy, and other people have mentioned it too. You sniff a lot."

"*What?*"

Wickes seemed to be restraining a smile. "I said you sniff a lot. You know—sniff instead of blowing your nose. At least you give that impression." Wickes squeezed the rubber ball hard.

"Oh God," Howard said with disgust.

"Okay, have it your way, Howard. Don't believe me if you don't want to. Go right on sniffing. You're undoubtedly used to it by now. You probably don't even realize you're doing it."

Howard by now was finding it hard to remain reasonable. Instead of being up in the sky, looking benignly down, he was right there on the train, seething. With great effort, he controlled his voice. "Bob," he said, "I'd like very much to think that this talk might have a good effect, that it's brought us closer together—but in all honesty I'm forced to doubt it." Howard got to his feet.

116

"Me too," Wickes said, putting the ball on the seat and spreading his newspaper wide again.

Howard went on down the aisle and found another seat.

Presently, without thinking, he pulled out his handkerchief and blew his nose hard.

* eleven

Howard thought it over and by the time the train reached Grand Central he had made a decision.

The hell with it, he decided.

In a headlong streak of honesty he had lost four friends, his emergency source of cigarettes, his tennis privileges and his aplomb. That was enough.

Wickes was a bastard and he had been totally justified in challenging his petty behavior, but it just wasn't worth it. His truth program was over.

Besides, good impulses didn't become him. There had been times when he was totally unrecognizable to himself. In posing as a man of truth he had been living a lie.

It was a beautiful morning, with scant humidity, a low pollution index and a satisfactory pollen count. Howard breathed deeply. On the way up Madison Avenue, he stopped for a pack of gum. Back out on the street, he opened the pack, took out a stick, stripped the wrapper and folded it into a wad which he cupped in his left hand. Striding along, arms swinging, looking innocently straight ahead, he dropped the wrapper on the sidewalk and kept going.

As for June, he would tell her nothing. She could go on thinking whatever she wanted to think, she and her idiot Group.

When Howard reached the office that morning, he gave himself a gold star.

"What's that one for?" June had handed him one from the box and watched as he licked it and stuck it on his chart.

"I can't tell you," he said. "You'll just have to take my word for it."

"That's fascinating," June said. "Things must be going well."

"They are," Howard said.

During the afternoon he called Charlotte and told her he wouldn't be home for dinner because he had to work with Malcolm Lorimer on the speech he was giving for Lorimer in Los Angeles.

In talking to Charlotte, he wasn't quite as smooth as he remembered himself. For one thing, he offered gratuitous information, which he had known for years was poor lying technique. "It's the lousiest speech I've ever read," he said unnecessarily. "It's incredible how lousy it is."

"You mean—he's already written it?"

Howard paused. "Yes, of course." He plunged ahead, making a comeback. "We worked on it yesterday until almost five o'clock trying to get some guts into it. It's so damned pious and mealy-mouthed you wouldn't believe it. I guess you can see what my problem is, can't you?"

"What's your problem, Howard?"

"Tact and diplomacy," he said. "I can't just come right out and *tell* him it's lousy. He has to see it for himself."

"Oh," Charlotte said.

That evening he picked up Sadie at Barney's Tavern and they took a taxi to her apartment. They got into bed immediately as they usually did, and Howard lay smoking while Sadie talked, telling him how much good it had done her to be home, saying that she had had a better relationship with her parents than at any time since the fifth grade. Howard felt his stomach muscles and listened. He wasn't particularly interested in what she was saying but he liked the soft sound of her voice, liked being where he was. Across the street there was a neon sign and it bathed the dimness with a faint pink glow, throwing a curved shadow on the ceiling. Howard looked up at the shadow, tapping his stomach muscles, liking the dim cavern where he now dwelt. In the dim rose light he could see her hair spread out over her pillow, and her features were moulded by the shadows. With the tip of his cigarette, he traced the curve of the shadow, looking up at the ceiling, tracing slowly and carefully, feeling contentment at the clean precise way he was tracing the shadow, feeling at home in the dark and deeply protected. At the moment there was nowhere else in the world that he wanted to be.

As she talked on and on, he started stroking her hair, thinking of all the things he loved about this desperate, vulnerable girl—her trust, her modesty, her guilt, her self-revilement, her sense or inadequacy, the tremendous importance she placed upon sex and upon sexual fantasies, the guileless way she believed what he told her, the fear she had of betraying ignorance before him. She was exactly what he needed. He would never give her up, never tell her the truth—the hell with June.

"My father had you investigated," Sadie said.

Howard moved his hand from his stomach muscles to his heart. "He did?"

"Yes."

"Hmmmm. Where?"

"He checked the CIA and the FBI and the State Department—he has a friend in the State Department. I wasn't going to tell you."

"What did he expect to find?" His voice now had the desired offhand sound.

"He wasn't looking for anything bad, Howard. He just wanted to see if they had any record of you—being there."

"And?"

"They didn't."

"Well . . . naturally . . ." Howard droned. He felt his heart again. "You know, of course, that Howard Jefferson is not my real name."

"Yes, of course, I know," Sadie said. "That's what I told him. He doesn't like the idea of my being in love with you— and not knowing your name."

Howard pulled her head to his shoulder. "I'm sorry, Sadie. If I could tell you, I would. You know that, don't you?"

"Oh, of course. That's what I told him. That if you could, you would."

"But I just can't, that's all. If mine were the only life at stake, it would be different . . ."

"I understand, I really do."

There was a range of the Blue Ridge mountains within sight of her home, and she started telling him about how she had felt when she looked at the mountains. Howard put out his cigarette. In a way that he knew she would find flattering, he said in a husky voice, "The hell with the mountains. I'm tired of hearing about the mountains. Let's talk about the ship, Sadie . . ." He pulled her close. "Okay?"

"Okay," she whispered. "But not the ship. I'm spread-eagled, Howard . . ."

"You're what?"

"I'm spread-eagled. My wrists are tied to stakes and my ankles are tied to stakes . . . with rawhide . . . thongs. And I'm right on the edge of a precipice, right on the edge of a deep canyon in Utah, only a few inches from the edge, and

I don't have any clothes on, but the sun is warm and I feel good because I know you're coming to get me. I'm an Indian girl and now I can see you galloping up on horseback. Your chest is bare and you don't have anything on except one of those breech cloths that flip up and you jump off your horse and you're ravishing me and I'm very happy, warm, happy . . . warm, happy . . . and my name is Running Deer . . . what's your name, Howard? . . . Oh, Howard, what's *your* name?"

"Spread Eagle—I mean Swift Eagle," Howard said.

It was 11:00, almost time to get up and go home. Sadie had fixed him a pizza and he sat propped up in bed, eating it. She insisted on keeping the lights off because she didn't want him to see how dirty the bedroom was. She kept the apartment a mess but he didn't hold it against her. He rather liked it because it seemed youthful and full of abandon, a titillating contrast to the antiseptic quality of Connecticut, to the meticulous way Charlotte kept house. There were times when he was stirred to pity. Sadie had only a very small closet and some of her dresses she hung on hooks. To see one of her dresses hanging on a hook, limp, helpless, miserable, full of guilt, downcast, expecting so little of the world—sometimes on the train he thought about it and moaned.

Now, with his mouth full, he said, "Sadie, there's one thing I want you to understand. I don't blame your father at all. In his place I think I'd have done the very same thing. In fact, I rather admire him for doing what he did. Okay?"

"Okay, Howard."

"But that sort of thing could get me into trouble. I mean it probably wouldn't—but it might."

"I understand," she said. "I told him not to do anything like that any more and he won't. He understands. He was just worried, that's all. About me. He worries about where I'm going and what I'm doing with my life. You understand, don't you?"

"Yes, of course. I understand."

"Anyway—something happened yesterday that may turn out to be a good break. My agent called me. Do you know where the Westport Playhouse is? Have you heard of it? It's a summer theater."

Howard was swallowing a final wad of pizza, determined not to choke. He waited. "In Connecticut?"

"Yes. There may be an opening. They're showing *Last of the Red Hot Lovers*—for a whole month, and one of the girls is pregnant. They're looking for a replacement. My agent wants me to go out there and audition. There's one thing that worries me about it."

Howard groped under the bed for his socks, then realized that he was too distracted to look for them. Sitting on the edge of the bed, he lit a cigarette. "What's that?"

"Well, if I got the part it would be for at least three weeks, maybe longer, and I know you wouldn't be able to come all the way out to Connecticut to see me."

"You mean—you'd live out there?"

"Yes. For whatever time I was in the play, I would. There's a big rooming house right in downtown Westport."

Howard put out his cigarette and then immediately reached for it, forgetting that he had put it out. Thinking of downtown Westport, he lit another one. "Are you sure it's a place where you'd want to spend a whole month of your life, Sadie?"

"Why not?"

"Well . . . why not indeed, I suppose . . ."

"It might be fun. It would be good experience. Do you know anything about Westport?"

"I've heard of it. It doesn't have a very good reputation."

"It doesn't?"

"Nope."

"Why not? I mean, in what way?"

Howard was silent. By now he was lying down again, looking up at the ceiling, beginning to trace, calling upon his brain
to come up with something. Sadie living in Westport for a
month! The risk was incalculable. He saw himself sneaking
home from the depot, skirting the downtown area. In fact
he'd have to get on and off the train at Norwalk.

"Well," he said, playing for time. "You'll have to take this
on faith. I can't really tell you *how* I know it. You understand . . ."

"Yes, of course. I understand. What is it?"

"Well . . ." Looking up at the ceiling, he started moving
his cigarette again. "There's a certain element . . ."

*. . . A certain filthy undercover white-slave element that
kidnaps young girls and sends them off to Mexico City mas-
sage parlors . . .*

In the long silence, Sadie waited expectantly. "That's all
you're going to tell me?" she asked finally. "That there's a
certain element?"

Again Howard tried. His mouth opened but nothing came
out. It should have been easy. She believed everything he told
her. She was absolutely convinced that he had his finger on
the pulse of the world and the underworld.

Howard was groping under the bed for his socks. "Yes,"
he said, "I guess that's really all I can tell you."

"Well gosh, Howard . . ." Sadie seemed dubious, as well
she might. "I'll have to think about it."

It was an unprecedented freeze-up—the first time ever in
his life that Howard Carew had tried to tell a lie and could
not.

✳ twelve

To Howard, for as long as the train ride home lasted, his freeze-up was a serious matter. He analyzed it in depth.

It was quite true that Sadie, after all her months of servitude at Barney's Tavern, deserved a crack at the acting job she so badly wanted—but he knew himself too well to believe that his reasons were altruistic.

It was also true that Sadie, considering the tenor of her fantasies, might have found the prospect of white slavery appealing—but this was an afterthought that didn't occur to him until he had dressed and left, hence it could have had no bearing upon his silence.

He remembered the words June had used on the morning when he rushed to the office and told her about the garbage can. How thrilled she had been. *Once you really start telling the truth, you won't be able to get along without it,* she had said, or words to that effect. *You won't be able to stop.*

Howard's head rested against the window. He opened his eyes, frowning. She was a spooky little bitch, but he didn't believe in spells. It had a much simpler explanation.

He tried to reconstruct what he had felt as he lay in the dark with Sadie waiting expectantly beside him. It was no spell. It was simply that something inside him didn't want to; wouldn't; couldn't. That's the way it had been.

He continued to worry. Lying was one thing and truth was another—but to lose his power of choice could be dangerous.

If a man put his big toe in the water he had every reason

to expect that if he wanted to he could pull it out again.

At breakfast next morning, he determined not to volunteer any information whatever about the speech that he and Lorimer were supposed to be working on.

Charlotte, however, put him to the test. Pouring herself a second cup of coffee, she asked:

"How did you and Mr. Lorimer make out with the speech last night?"

Howard nodded. "Fine." He smiled, taking heart from the firm resonance of his voice. "I think I finally got him to see things my way."

"Good," Charlotte said.

Howard conceded that it was a minor test. There was no major test until Saturday when he was called upon to handle his first real estate assignment since the evening with the young Thompsons.

Richard Traynor, head of Venture Realty, was a man who came as close to crookedness as he possibly could without actually violating the law. Although he stopped short of outright fraud, he was a master of deceit, a ruthless, swaggering old pirate, utterly contemptuous of the public. Traynor was a retired navy captain who had been "passed over" for admiral, and he ran his real estate agency as he might have run a ship, insisting that he be addressed as Captain Traynor rather than Mr. Traynor, demanding split-second punctuality and all-out, truth-shading performance. Still in his early sixties, he had made, in his retirement years, a great deal of money which he didn't need, since his wife was loaded in her own right, but rich as he was he continued to play the profit game with grim, unrelenting greed—and he was a very bad loser. It was as though each new sales prospect in turn personified the navy board which had deemed him unfit for the rank of admiral, passed him over, and sent him off to early retirement.

Traynor, as the real estate saying had it, would sell termites to his own mother, and from his employees he expected the same light regard for sales ethics.

After lunch Howard headed down to Westport, bound for the office of Venture Realty. By now he was calm. He felt confident he could handle whatever had to be handled without making a fool of himself. It was true that in his present mood he was probably incapable of the artificiality he had visited upon the young Thompsons, but neither would he risk losing his job. In the final analysis, his behavior would be determined in large measure by the type of client who showed up. A seasoned realtor matched his own mood and personality to the mood and personality of the prospect.

Howard found the prospect, or prospects, waiting in the office of Traynor's secretary, a frail, fluttery redhead named Miss Coe, whose nerves were badly shot from long years of association with Traynor. Because she had a bad head cold that day, Miss Coe seemed even more fluttery than usual, and her speech was nasal.

"Mr. and Mrs. Marble," she said, "this is our Mr. Carew. Howard, Mr. and Mrs. Marble are interested in the Hansen house. Now just let me get the key for you . . ." With her back to the Marbles, she gave Howard a look that mystified him as she disengaged the key from the rack beside her desk.

Mr. Marble was dark with heavy brows beneath a camel's hair cap. He wore a light blue sweater, zippered half way, and beneath it a black-and-white checkered shirt. His rather baggy green trousers matched his green suede desert boots.

Mrs. Marble was a tiny blonde with large blue eyes. The taut skin of her face suggested plastic surgery. She wore a tweed suit and was smoking a slim cigar.

"We can all sit in front," Howard said as he led them to his car.

HOWARD'S BAG

Mr. Marble said he would sit in back, that Mrs. Marble could sit in front. Howard helped them in and, having fought free of the Saturday afternoon Westport traffic, they were soon tooling along toward the uplands, over winding roads dappled with crisp shadows thrown by the bright August sun. The day could not have been more beautiful. The air was warm and dry. It was Connecticut at its finest, the sort of day, Howard thought, when anything might look good, even the Hansen house. "Are you folks new to Connecticut?" he asked as they rolled along. It was a question that was often helpful in taking the measure of a client.

"Thank God, yes," Mr. Marble muttered from the back seat.

"Yes, we are," Mrs. Marble said, tossing her slim cigar from the window and lighting another.

"Well, it's a lovely state," Howard said. "At least we in Connecticut think so." He chuckled.

In the rearview mirror, he glanced at Marble's reflection. The bill of his cap had come unsnapped and had fallen low over his brow. The word Mafia flitted through Howard's mind. Not, he thought, with a name like Marble, and for Marble to be an assumed name was unlikely because Mafia members were proud of their names and kept them, so he had read.

"There are two things you should know about us," Mrs. Marble said. Howard glanced at her and then looked back at the road. She could have been anywhere from forty-five to sixty. "First," she said, "my husband is very impatient. He's a quick decision-maker. The second thing is that we don't know very much about houses. Now you'll probably think that's a funny thing for me to say . . ."

"Well . . ." Howard ventured.

There was no reply.

"You probably won't believe it," Mrs. Marble said, "but

127

Jimmy has never lived in a house in his life. Always either apartments or hotels."

"So now she wants a house," Marble said.

"I lived in a house once when I was a little girl," Mrs. Marble said. "And I never forgot it. A very, very old house."

She fell silent. "Well," Howard said carefully, still taking their measure, "the Hansen house is something I think you may find—interesting." He paused. "It's a two-story, white clapboard, two acres; of course, everything is zoned two acres . . ."

"We won't be in it much." Marble yawned. "What's the price?"

"Sixty-nine, nine-fifty," Howard said.

"You might as well say seventy thou, then?"

"Close," Howard agreed. "It was owned by a retired department store executive and I think you'll find it very interesting—some of the things he did to the interior."

"The girl back there at the office said it was a very old house," Mrs. Marble said.

"That's correct," Howard said. "It is quite old."

Howard by now had pretty well exhausted his store of knowledge, for the fact was that although he had driven by the house many times he had never been inside and had never shown it to a prospect. Captain Traynor, however, had an exclusive on it, had spent money advertising it for almost a year and burned with a fierce flame to get it sold. A notation on the listing card, for company eyes only, said, "Keep clients out of cellar if possible." The words "if possible" had then been inked out. The house was truly old, what Traynor persisted in calling "one of our heirloom pieces," and the cellar, from all reports, was a dungeon-keep. Its cement surface, according to one of the other salesmen, had long since worn thin and crumbled into fine powder, so that the floor was more dirt than cement, and it had also at one time been infested with termites. These had long ago been exterminated and hence the house could legitimately be warranted as termite-free, yet there had been termite damage to some of the beams.

Along with all these features, the house also had a pronounced architectural eccentricity which became apparent as they now entered a short lane and looped around to the front doorway, a beautifully ornate doorway with a scrolled pediment and an aureole of blue glass (which Traynor claimed was the only glass of its kind in Connecticut, the sort of statement he was given to making and the sort which was extremely difficult to disprove). The doorway was centered. What was architecturally strange was that the broad expanse of white clapboard on the left was a blank wall, containing not a single window. On the right there were two windows downstairs and two upstairs. Of this phenomenon, however, the Marbles made no mention.

"Would you be commuting to New York, Mr. Marble?" Howard asked as they got out of the car.

"Whenever I happen to be here, yeah," said Marble.

"Well, it's no great distance to the train from here," Howard said.

"Train? What train?"

"Jimmy would be driving to New York," Mrs. Marble said. "I mean, be driven, that is."

"Oh," Howard said. "Well . . ." He took the key from his pocket. "Let's go in, shall we?"

"Do we have to?" Marble asked.

"Oh, Jimmy . . ." Mrs. Marble giggled. "You can't just look at the outside. After all . . ."

"So you want a house, I buy you a house." Yawning, Marble pointed. "This is a house."

Howard, listening intently, was having trouble with the lock. When he finally managed to turn the key, the door would not yield. He gave it a good push with the heel of his hand. Still it did not budge. "I guess it's stuck a little," he said.

"That's okay," Marble said. "Whenever we come we'll remember to bring a football team with us." He made a clicking sound with his tongue.

Howard gave the door a shoulder and all his weight. It opened. "There we go," he said. The damp cold of the interior rushed to meet them. "Heat hasn't been on, of course," he said. "And we've had some chilly nights."

"Personally you can take every house ever built and shove it," Marble said.

"I think there's a time when people should have a house," Mrs. Marble said.

"I need a house like I need the clap," said Marble.

Howard waited a second or two and then chuckled.

"House interferes with your life," Marble said. "So . . . I'll buy you a house, what the hell. I'll level with you, Mr. Grew. You could tell me this house is worth a hundred thou and I wouldn't know any different. So—where's all these interesting things the department store guy did?"

In saying that the interior contained things of interest, Howard was being very general. Casting about, he pointed out the drift-wood panelling in the windowless living room and he also found, mounted in the wall, two large dial faces, one registering the wind direction and the other the wind velocity.

"Hey!" Marble seemed interested. "The wind's from the northwest and it's seven miles an hour. Hey! Baby! Come 'ere a minute! Look, for God's sake!"

"Ummmm," Mrs. Marble said.

"The owner left these for the new owners," Howard said.

"I wonder why he did that," Marble said.

"I suppose because—I just couldn't say," Howard replied.

"Perhaps because he felt he would have no further use for them."

"Maybe the son of a bitch moved where they don't *have* any wind." Marble made the clicking sound with his tongue again.

"Oh, Jimmy . . ." His wife giggled.

"Dishwasher and garbage disposer," Howard said, moving on. "And here off the kitchen there's a utility room with a washer and a drier."

"We have those in the apartment," Marble said. "Put a couple of quarters in and you can wash and dry till you go crazy."

Howard led them through the remainder of the house, upstairs and down, thinking occasionally of the basement.

Mrs. Marble walked through in a daze, admiring everything she saw. Mr. Marble followed in a different sort of daze, as if he saw nothing.

When they came to a stop in the center hallway, Marble said, "Okay, okay, how much did you say?"

"Sixty-nine thousand, nine-hundred and fifty dollars," Howard replied.

Marble nodded, then shrugged.

It was at this point, according to sales psychology, that Howard was supposed to say the house had just come on the market, that it was certain to be snapped up in a hurry, and that a firm offer of $65,000 had already been turned down.

He said none of it.

"Will you excuse us just a second?" Mrs. Marble asked.

"Certainly," Howard said.

The Marbles withdrew into the kitchen and began conversing in low tones. Twice Howard heard Mrs. Marble giggle and say, "Oh, Jimmy!"

While they were gone, Howard did some figuring. At,

say, sixty thousand, his share of the commission would be $1,800.

"Oh, the hell with it," he heard Marble mutter. "Let's get it over with. Already I'm worn out from house-hunting."

Howard turned. He had heard the sound of a car outside and his instinct was to look from the window, but since he was in the living room there were no windows to look from. He reached the front door just as it was butted open by none other than Captain Traynor, wearing a dark blue blazer, a tightly knotted black tie and a stiff white collar. From his flushed face and the look in his small demonic eyes, he was hot on the spoor. He raised a hand in a half-salute, as was his custom. "Where are your people?" he asked.

"In the kitchen," Howard said in a voice involuntarily conspiratorial.

Traynor frowned. With delicate fingers, he touched his thinning white, slicked-down hair. "Talking?" he asked, also conspiratorially.

Howard nodded.

It was at this point that the Marbles emerged. "Okay, we'll take it," Marble said.

In moments of high excitement, Traynor was given to making staccato humming noises, and he did so now.

"I told you Jimmy likes to do things in a hurry," Mrs. Marble said.

Howard smiled. "Mr. and Mrs. Marble—Captain Traynor. Captain Traynor is president of our company."

"Mrs. Marble . . ." Traynor bowed from the waist, heels together. "Mr. Marble . . ." He shook Marble's hand and then gave him a semi-salute, brushing the bill of Marble's cap, which thereupon came unsnapped again and fell low over his brow. "Oops!"

"He asked me to *marry* him thirteen hours after we met," Mrs. Marble said.

"Really?" Howard smiled.

"Remarkable," Traynor said with one of his very phoniest grins.

"Today's our anniversary," Mrs. Marble said.

"Congratulations." Howard said.

"We've been married three weeks today," Mrs. Marble said.

"Remarkable," Traynor said, not listening. "Congratulations indeed," he said, giving another half-salute. "Howard, did I hear these good people say they were ready to make an offer on this charming old home?" He smiled. "I think I did indeed."

"What do I do, give a deposit or what?" Marble asked. He had by now withdrawn a blank check from his wallet and was pounding his zippered sweater as if in search of a writing instrument.

A ball-point pen glided from Traynor's inside jacket pocket to Marble's hand.

"So how much?" Marble asked.

"Ten percent deposit should do nicely," said Traynor. "Ah . . . what was your offer, may I ask?"

"What it costs," Marble said.

"Jimmy doesn't like to haggle," said Mrs. Marble.

"Seventy thou minus fifty bucks is the way I make it, isn't that what you said, Mr. Grew?"

"Indeed," said Captain Traynor.

"That's right," Howard said.

"Aaaaaah . . . about financing," Traynor said.

"Whaddya mean?" Marble asked. "Financing?"

"Jimmy always likes to pay cash," Mrs. Marble explained.

"Hell yes," Marble said. "Unless you take American Express. You take American Express?"

Traynor gave an imitation of a hearty laugh.

"Well then, cash," Marble said. "I hate paying interest."

Howard by now was in the living room, looking at the wind velocity dial. He returned to the hallway in time to see Traynor do a little skip. And then as Marble cast about for a writing surface and as Traynor obligingly pointed to a radiator cover, Mrs. Marble asked a question.

"You're sure now, Jimmy?"

"Let's get it over with," Marble said.

"You're sure you've seen everything you'd like to see?"

Marble turned from the radiator cover. "What else *is* there to see, for God's sake? We've seen it all. We've *been* here half our married life."

"You're sure you don't want to have a look at the attic?" Mrs. Marble asked.

"Aha, there *is* no attic," Traynor said swiftly and truthfully. "No attic whatsoever. You might think there was an attic but there's *not*."

"Good," Mrs. Marble said. "What a relief. I hate attics and I hate basements. Oh—is there a basement?"

"A what?" Traynor asked.

Mrs. Marble had addressed her question not to Traynor—but to Howard. "A basement?" Howard asked.

"Yes," Mrs. Marble said.

Howard ran a hand over his head. He was aware of Traynor's rapid breathing, his high tension, his darting eyes. He hesitated not at all. "Yes," he replied. "There is a basement."

"Oh," Mrs. Marble said. "There is?"

"Yes," Howard said.

Traynor experienced a paroxysm of coughing which he quickly aborted. His face was florid, his body began to move this way and that and he gave a half-salute to the wall.

"What's down there?" Mrs. Marble asked. "I hate basements."

"And I don't for one minute blame you, ma'am," Traynor

said. "My wife feels exactly the same way. Actually there's *nothing* down there except the heating plant—a very good one by the way."

Marble had turned to listen, leaving the still blank check and the ball point pen on the radiator cover.

"A whole heating plant?" he asked. "For just one lousy house?"

Traynor looked at him uncertainly. "As Howard probably told you," he said, "the house is warranted absolutely free of termites."

"*Termites?*" Marble thrust his cap on the back of his head.

"They're like little flying ants, honey," Mrs. Marble said.

"So what's with the termites?" Marble asked. "What do they do?"

"They eat a house up," Mrs. Marble said.

"Well they sure as hell didn't eat *this* one up," Marble said. "Because here it is. Right here. Okay. Look. Is it a good basement or not? That's all I want to know."

"Perfectly good," Traynor said. "If you've seen one basement you've seen them all." He chuckled. "At least that's the way my wife feels about it. How about yours, Howard?" He turned to Howard and for a brief moment his eyes glittered with sheer hatred.

"My what?" Howard asked.

"Your *wife.*"

"What about her?" Howard asked.

"Absolutely termite-free," Traynor said. "Which is the big point."

"Mr. Grew's wife is absolutely termite-free, I'll remember that," Marble said, shuffling spiritedly.

"Oh, Jimmy," Mrs. Marble said.

"So where are we?" Marble said. "You know something, you guys? Sometimes I get these distinct impressions about

human beings, and what I'm getting is a distinct impression
that the captain here thinks it's a good cellar—and Mr. Grew,
he thinks it's *not* such a good cellar. So who's right?"

"For my money, a cellar is a cellar," Traynor said.

"Maybe we better look at the cellar," Marble said. "I mean,
I don't *wanna* look at the cellar, but maybe I'd *better* look
at the cellar. So . . . can we look at the cellar?"

Although Traynor tried to give his reply a note of hearty
assurance, it came out a dirge. "Of course you can look at the
cellar," he wailed. "Lead the way, Howard."

As they jockeyed for position toward the cellar doorway,
Traynor managed to slip Howard another look of hatred.
Howard opened the door and started down. A distinct odor
of damp earth came rushing up the stairway. "Smells like a
tomb," he heard Marble say from the head of the steps. "You
first, Jimmy," Mrs. Marble said. "I'm scared."

Traynor's chuckle was a patronizing comment on the help-
lessness of woman.

Groping overhead, Howard grabbed a string and pulled.
A naked bulb lit up, casting a dim light. The oil burner
loomed large in the shadows.

Slowly down the steps came the Marbles. "That other
owner, he was strictly a fifteen-watt bulb man," Marble said.
"Hey, what's with the floor? That's a helluva looking floor,
Mr. Grew. Nothing but dirt."

Overhead there was a loud noise, as if someone were jumping up and down and then kicking a wall. A few seconds
later, Traynor came pounding down the steps.

"I'll see if I can find another light," Howard said, peering
about the ceiling.

"Plenty of light, plenty of light," Traynor said. "Now you
see," he said, pointing at the oil burner, "here you have your
heating plant."

"The floor's lousy," Marble said. "I know enough about floors to know the floor's lousy."

"Actually," Traynor said, "in point of fact, a great deal could be done with this basement. It could be a bang-up rumpus room."

"It's spooky," Mrs. Marble said.

"Let's find another light," Marble said. "Here." He pulled another string and a second bulb cast a ghostly light. "Now look at this floor . . ." He scraped at it with his desert boot. "What the hell *was* this floor, Mr. Grew?"

"It was originally paved with cement," Howard said. "But now it's gone back to dirt, more or less."

"Gone to earth!" Marble said and howled, as if he were a fox.

"Oh, Jimmy," Mrs. Marble said.

"I suppose you know all there is to be known about oil burners," Traynor was saying. "Now here, Mr. Marble, here's your water temperature."

"*Where's* my water temperature?" Marble asked. "The hell with the water temperature. I'm still trying to get the big picture."

On the foundation wall, Howard saw a telltale vertical line, slightly discolored, where once a termite tunnel had climbed.

"Throw a little cement down and paint the walls," Traynor was saying. "Here's where your bar could be, with a few bar stools, put up a couple of port-and-starboard running lights for atmosphere. Say!"

"What?" Alarmed, Marble looked over his shoulder. "What is it, for God's sake?"

"Oh, say!" Traynor said. "I just happened to think! I've got a spare set of running lights I'd be glad to let you have, I mean as a gift. I have no further use for them."

"You sure?" Marble asked.

"Sure as rain."

"God!" Marble paused. "Running lights."

"Yes. Port and starboard. Exactly."

"Say!" Marble said.

Traynor chuckled. He was making a comeback. "You may be wondering, of course, why Mr. Hansen left the basement this way."

"That's one of the things I've been wondering," Marble said.

"Actually for verisimilitude."

"Write that down, baby," Marble said.

"This, of course," Traynor went on, "being one of your very old houses, a real heirloom piece. He didn't want to do anything that would destroy the authenticity."

"Well, he did a damned good job of it," Marble said. "What's that you're doing, Mr. Grew?"

Howard had been looking closely at one of the overhead beams and now found that he was scratching at it with his fingernail. The wood was pulpy and he had scratched away a half-inch or so. "I'm scratching this beam with my fingernail," he said.

"That's an execllent way to get a broken fingernail," Traynor said.

"Is that what the termites did?" Mrs. Marble asked with excitement. "Is it, Mr. Grew?"

"Yes," Howard said.

"Well those dirty little bastards," Marble said.

"Where? Where?" Traynor strode over and glowered up at the beam. "As I told you before, this house is warranted absolutely *free* of termites."

Marble now scratched at the beam with his own fingernail, flaking away some of the wood. "Is that dangerous?" he asked.

"Hah!" Traynor's laugh was tolerant.

"Mr. Grew?" Marble asked. "Would that board have to be replaced, say?"

"Not necessarily," Howard said. "If you wanted to, you could have another beam spliced in right next to this one."

"God Almighty!" Marble said. "I don't wanna splice beams. I just wanna buy a house."

"Exactly!" Traynor laughed in triumph. "Exactly! Those beams are good for many many years, good for a whole lot longer than *I* am." He chuckled.

"Yeah," Marble said, "but you don't have to stand down here and hold the house up."

"They look like the original beams," Traynor said. "See? They have that hand-adzed look, extremely valuable, very rare and just as solid as steel."

"Yes, they are hand-hewn," Howard agreed.

"How often do you find a house with hand-hewn beams?" Traynor demanded.

"Me?" Marble asked.

"Now you see, Mrs. Marble," Traynor said, taking her arm. "Where I had in mind for the bar was right over here, standing out a little apart from the wall, of course. It could be like an old Revolutionary War tavern. It's amazing what a little taste and imagination can do for a place, and I can tell that you and Mr. Marble are people of taste and imagination."

"No," Marble said.

"I beg your pardon?" Traynor asked.

"It's a funny thing about me and the wife," Marble said. "We don't have very much taste and we don't have very much imagination either. So where would that leave us?"

Traynor laughed uncertainly. "Well, you certainly look like people of taste and imagination to *me*," he said. "Now you see—come over here a second, Mr. Marble, and stand right here, behind the bar, where the bar would be. That's right. Now you approach the bar, Mrs. Marble—see?"

"I get it," Marble said. "I'm here tending bar and somebody comes up and asks for a drink, and I give them whatever they ask for. We've got the running lights on, and we got pretzels and potato chips on the bar, and people are smoking and drinking and talking about the stock market and telling dirty jokes, we got some music going, everybody's having a helluva good time . . ."

"Exactly," Traynor said. "*Exactly*."

"I'm beginning to feel it," Marble said. "What's that loose brick over there in the corner?"

"Where?" Traynor asked.

"Right there."

"Oh. Well, just an extra brick, I suppose."

Marble approached the brick and gave it a kick, revealing a hole about four inches in diameter. "I'll be damned," he said. "You know what it looks like? It looks like a rat-hole, right in the floor!"

"Nonsense," Traynor howled.

"Don't tell me, Captain," Marble said. "I lived in the city my whole life, at least I know what a rat-hole looks like. It must be because of the dirt floor. The bastard must have tunneled right under the foundation and come up right in the floor. Sometimes they'll do that. Follow a pipe up. Well I'll be damned."

Mrs. Marble, having already shrieked, was now making for the stairway.

Traynor's demeanor became grave, even scholarly. "Now I'll tell you something," he said. "As I say, this is one of your very old houses, a real heirloom piece, and if memory serves it was used during the Civil War as part of the underground railway for fugitive slaves, and if memory serves—"

"Whoa!" Marble said. "Whoa, Cap'n. Hold it right there.

If a slave came up through that hole, it's gotta be one helluva small slave!"

So saying, Marble headed for the stairway, with Traynor close behind. "On something like this, Mr. Marble," he said as they climbed the steps, "you don't want to make the mistake of not being able to see the woods for the trees. It's your decision, of course, but I'd hate like the very mischief to see you and your good wife make a mistake . . ."

Howard lingered behind to pull the light cords. As he was doing so, he heard a repeated thumping sound that seemed to come from the direction of the front door.

By the time he got upstairs, Mrs. Marble had managed to yank open the door and was headed for the great outdoors.

Marble plucked his blank check from the radiator cover and followed her, with Traynor close behind, still talking of the woods and the trees.

About 5:00 that afternoon, with Charlotte still not home from a day of shopping, Howard lay in the den watching a stock car race on television when he heard an explosive roar of a motorcycle and then a heavy knock at the front door. He opened it to find a young man in blue denim jeans and matching jacket. "You Mr. Carew?" Howard took the envelope that was offered, and the young man got back on his motorcycle and roared off. The envelope was addressed, "H. Carew." He opened it and read:

> Carew:
> I need hardly tell you that your association with Venture Realty is henceforth and forever terminated, you damned idiot.
> > Richard Traynor
> > Captain, USN (ret)

✴ thirteen

Because his own moral position had always been so weak, Howard rarely in his adult life had known the luxury of righteous indignation. Now he felt it.

What had he done wrong? He had been asked a direct question: "Is there a basement?" All he had done was reply: "Yes, there is a basement."

What kind of world was it where simple honesty could bring such petty vindictiveness?

Howard picked up the phone in a rage, jabbing at the digits of Traynor's home number. "Look, Traynor," he began, "let's get one thing straight. I don't need your damned job. I don't even want it—"

"Well, you don't have it," Traynor barked and thereupon hung up.

Immediately Howard dialed the number again. It was busy. He jammed down the phone. As he did so it rang. "Hello," he snapped.

"It might interest you to know," Traynor said, "that the client you drove off, Jimmy Marble, is one of the foremost television producers in the United States."

Traynor hung up. Howard dialed him again. The line was busy and it remained busy throughout the evening.

Charlotte, when he told her, didn't seem particularly concerned. "You don't really need an extra job," she said. "We can get along fine on what you make, plus what I get occasionally for my paintings. Isn't that true?" She looked at him. "Isn't that true, Howard?"

Howard grunted.

But on Monday he stayed home from the office. That day in all he covered nine real estate offices, ranging south to Norwalk, north to Bridgeport, and west to Danbury, laying eggs as he went. In some places he did not get past the receptionist, in three he got to the head of the agency, and although he encountered no overt discourtesy he did detect a certain slyness, enough to make him suspect that his fame had gone before him.

The thing to realize was that in dealing with Traynor he was dealing with a lunatic. Even so he knew he could not rest until he had pressed the matter as far as it would press. June agreed with him. "It's your moral duty," she said.

But he needed no encouragement. Truth and honesty as a project no longer claimed his attention. All that he cared about was that he had been wronged.

On Wednesday morning at 9:15, bestowing a grim smile on the aghast Miss Coe, he strode past her desk into Captain Traynor's office.

"Traynor," he said, "there's something I'd like to get straight with you, buddy."

Traynor's eyes glittered fiercely. He seemed dumbfounded. What was happening to him could only be happening in civilian life, never in the Navy. Everything about him indicated a yearning to have Howard keelhauled, or flogged through the fleet.

"See here, Carew . . ." He rose from his chair and immediately sat down again. "Don't think you can come down here apologizing. You could push a peanut with your nose all the way to Youngstown, Ohio, and I still wouldn't give you your job back."

"I didn't come to apologize, and I don't want my job back." By now Howard's anger had crystallized into icy contempt, and it was in this mood that he had approached the confrontation.

"Well, what is it you want, before I call the police . . . I've got a good mind to have Miss Coe toss you right out."

Uninvited, Howard sat down in the black and gold rocker, painted by Traynor's wife to give the office a Colonial air. Scornfully he glanced at a framed citation on the wall above Traynor's sleek, silvered, greasy cap of hair. It proclaimed Traynor "Realtor of the Year."

"You're a disgrace," Howard said. "You're a blight."

Traynor would not permit his ears to hear. "I just don't know what life is coming to any more." He was looking all around the ceiling. "Here's a man who's violated every known precept of decency and professional ethics, coming right here into my office! What is it you want, Carew?"

"*Decency? Professional ethics?* My God, Traynor! The woman asked me if the house had a basement. I said yes, that it did have a basement."

"Which was totally and utterly unnecessary," Traynor said. "You knew full well, Carew, how desperately I wanted to get that house sold. And there was a man with a pen in his hand, ready to sign a check for sixty-nine thousand, nine hundred and fifty dollars . . ." Traynor was making the buzzing and humming noises that he always made when he was excited, particularly when he was excited about money. "And not content with that, you have to start scraping beams with your fingernail, calling his attention to termite damage! My God, man! If money means nothing to you—if you have no need to earn your daily bread, then at least have some regard for those who do!"

"I'll give that statement the contempt that it deserves," Howard said. "You had no right to fire me. And you have no right to ruin my reputation with other real estate offices, and if you keep it up I'll have you sued for character assassination." Howard got to his feet with a feeling of satisfaction. "You should be drummed out of the real estate industry."

Traynor was pointing a finger at his chest. "Miss Coe! See this man out!" Again Traynor rose and again sat down immediately. "You're just typical, Carew, absolutely typical of today's working man—absolutely no regard for the function of the entrepreneur who gives him his job and provides the risk-capital and offers him his God-given opportunity to earn his daily bread!"

Howard looked at Traynor with amazement, realizing he meant every word he had said.

"Captain Traynor," he said quietly, "I think you're insane."

Turning, he strode triumphantly out.

"Miss Coe!" Traynor howled. "See that this man leaves the premises immediately! I hate you, Carew!"

"He's already left them," Miss Coe replied as Howard slammed the door behind him.

The very next night Howard and Charlotte were at dinner when the telephone rang. Howard answered. "Hello," a male voice said. "I'm calling to arrange a date. How much do you need to know about me?"

"I beg your pardon," Howard said.

"I'm thirty-five, single, about five-seven . . ."

"You must have the wrong number," Howard said and hung up.

"What was that?" Charlotte asked.

"Wrong number." Howard sat down again. He frowned. "Some guy wanting to arrange a date."

The telephone rang again. Howard answered. "Hello." It was the same caller. "Is this 226-3098?"

"That's right."

"Well, is this the Esquire Dating Service?"

"No, it is *not*," Howard said. "My God!"

"I have your ad—"

"I didn't place any ad," Howard said. "What ad?"

"A classified ad in this morning's paper. It gives this number."

"Son of a bitch!" Howard said.

"Look now, don't get nasty, all—"

"I wasn't calling you a son of a bitch," Howard explained. "I was just using it as an expletive. Look, would you mind reading me what the ad says?"

"I have it right here. It says, 'Lonely? Call Esquire Dating Service. Contacts arranged. Complete satisfaction. Call after seven P.M.' Then it gives this number."

"Well, there's been a mistake," Howard said. "It's the wrong number. This is not any Esquire Dating Service. It's a private residence. Please don't call again."

He hung up and stood for a moment, lost in thought, frowning. "Some son of a bitch has given our phone number as the number of a dating bureau. It's in a classified ad. Traynor, I'd be willing to bet."

Charlotte looked pained. "How could he *do* that?"

"I guess he just paid his money and placed it, that's all. Newspapers don't check up, they just take the money and print it." The telephone rang. "Oh my God!" Howard snatched up the phone. "*Hello!*" he barked. "No, this is *not* the Esquire Dating Service. The number in the paper was a wrong number."

The caller this time was female. "I know what you're doing," she said. "I can always tell right away."

"Tell what?" Howard demanded. "I'm not trying to do *anything* except eat my supper."

Her voice was a soft lament. "You think I'm not attractive. How can you tell over the telephone how attractive I am?"

Howard was touched with pity. "Listen," he said, "I'm terribly sorry but it's all a mistake. This is a private residence and the phone number in the classified ad was wrong. You have the wrong number—no matter what the ad says . . . Yes, I'm sure you *do* have a pleasant personality, I can tell by your voice . . . Say your name? . . . Okay . . . Okay, hello, Mickey . . ." Holding the phone against his chest, Howard looked at Charlotte with anguish. "Yes," he said, lifting it to his ear again. "Yes, I'm sure you are . . . Well, that's something, of course, that I'd have no way of knowing . . ."

Howard's expression changed abruptly. His eyebrows shot up. "No, I really couldn't . . . No, I'll have to take your word for it . . . Yes . . . Well, that's a very—unusual accomplishment, but I'm afraid there's nobody at this number who can help you. Good night."

Howard hung up. "You must have made him awfully angry," Charlotte said.

"Who?"

"Captain Traynor."

"The old bastard." Howard by now was considering other candidates. Wickes, for example. "I'd better take it off the hook before it rings again," he said.

For three evenings, beginning promptly at seven, the telephone rang repeatedly until one or the other took it off the hook. The paper involved, Howard discovered, was not the local paper after all, but a Long Island paper. His only recourse was to the telephone company. He asked for and was assigned a new telephone number. The old one was retired. They had had the same number ever since they built the house, and he felt he was saying farewell to an era.

On Saturday afternoon of that week he and Charlotte, having duly made their reservation in advance, took the long long trip to the public tennis courts, played their allotted hour and then made the long trip home.

They arrived to find on their front lawn a rusted automobile engine, an antique gas range and an old white refrigerator without a door.

Leaning against the front stoop was a huge Pepsi-Cola machine.

For a few moments they sat dumbfounded, unable to get out of the car.

"Oh, Howard . . . *Howard* . . ." Charlotte seemed in pain.

Howard sat there, grimly stoic. Finally he got out. Together they advanced over the lawn. After a brief glance at the stove, Howard veered off. He stood staring at the trunk of a birch tree, thinking scrap iron, thinking Harry Allison.

He turned to find Charlotte staring at the Pepsi-Cola machine with horror, as if it were something grotesque and monstrous, which of course it was. "Howard, really . . . you've got to *do* something. This has to stop."

"What the hell do you want me to do—pick it up and throw it away?" Howard walked slowly across the lawn and circled the automobile engine, looking at it from various angles. Tentatively he tried to lift it, then backed away.

In late afternoon, after consulting the yellow pages of the phone book, he arranged with an outfit called Ace Haul to get rid of the unwelcome items for the sum of fifty dollars. Ace Haul promised to get to it as soon as possible, but in no case sooner than Monday.

After supper Howard sat on his terrace in the evening light, gazing out over the meadow, still raging over the items on the lawn. A dirt road ran abreast of the meadow. In the distance it made a right angle turn, bounding the meadow on the north and east. Two kids and a large brown dog were running down the road, making the turn.

Charlotte came out, stood beside him for a moment, patted

his head and went back in. Watching the kids and the dog and having Charlotte pat his head made him feel calmer. Once past her initial reaction, Charlotte hadn't been nearly as upset about the unwelcome gifts as he might have expected, and this surprised him. If he was growing more mature, so then was she. By now she knew all about his confrontations with Sattersbee, with Wickes and even with Cookie Allison, and she seemed to take them in stride. She seemed to be aware that he was undergoing changes. Occasionally he had caught her regarding him with a look of curiosity, of appraisal. Often now in passing she would touch his shoulder or pat his head, as she just had, or let her hand trail lingeringly over his shoulder, a gesture that seemed full of affection but which went even beyond affection, into the area of compassion and understanding.

From Charlotte his thoughts turned to Sadie, just as so often his thoughts turned from Sadie to Charlotte. He was beginning to feel guilty about Sadie because he hadn't seen her and hadn't called her. When he went a long time without calling her, she automatically assumed that he was overseas. She of course could not call him, one reason being that she didn't know who he was. Neither did he. He wasn't sure whether he was a poseur or a man in the process of going straight.

These were his thoughts when he heard Charlotte call from the living room:

"Howard, Fred just drove in."

✷ fourteen

Howard's father had died young, leaving Fred the head of the family, a position which, far from finding burdensome, he accepted with great relish. Taking over at the age of twenty-two or so, he had continued to relish it right up to the present.

Just past fifty and youthful for his age, Fred was a solid citizen who lived by the time-tested formulas of life. Although he lived by convention, he also found it necessary to laugh at convention, thus creating an impression of broad-mindedness to go with his rock-solid conventionality. There were times when Howard told himself that Fred had absolutely no idea what he really did believe, perhaps a family trait.

Fred had married his high school sweetheart and for many years he had made proud and frequent mention of the fact. These were the years when marrying one's high school sweetheart seemed a good, solid, American thing to do, even somewhat colorful. In recent years Fred hadn't mentioned it at all.

For Howard, Fred had deep affection, which often took the form of kidding. Putting it another way, he kidded Howard a great deal and claimed that he did so out of deep affection.

It was twilight when Fred arrived. Hearing Charlotte announce his arrival, Howard went into the living room. As he did so, he heard Fred outside, calling, "Yoo hoo." It occurred to Howard that Saturday evening was a strange time for Fred to drop by.

The front door stood open, and through the screen door he

could see Fred still outside, inspecting the automobile engine, smiling, then passing on to have a look at the refrigerator. Spotting Howard at the screen door, he approached with solemnity. "Pardon me," he said, "I'm looking for the Bide-a-wee Durable Consumer Goods Shop—can you help me?" Howard stepped outside as Fred moved to the Pepsi-Cola machine. "Hey, Howard," he said, reaching into his pocket, "do you have change for a quarter?" Laughing, he clapped Howard on the shoulder and tapped him in the stomach with his knuckles. "Well, old buddy, certainly a nice place you have here." Hearing Charlotte inside, he pressed his nose to the screen door and looked in. "Yoo hoo," he said.

"Hello, Fred," Charlotte said. "Come in."

Fred opened the screen door and Howard followed him in. Catching sight of Charlotte, Fred drew back and cocked his head to one side. "Well, hel-*lo*." He stepped forward and kissed her on the lips. Fred considered himself suave with women. Charlotte said his kisses were wet.

"Well . . ." Fred grinned from one to the other. "Tell me . . . how are things?"

Fred still had all his hair. It was just as dark and just as slickly parted as it had been back in the days when he was president of his high school fraternity—and the lothario of sorority row. He was wearing what he considered his best tweed jacket, heather in shade and looking straight out of the moors of Scotland. No less than three times in the preceding year he had told Howard it cost him two hundred fifty dollars. He wore it in hot weather and cold. Howard noticed with pleasure that it was far too big for him, hung on him like a sack.

Charlotte had asked Fred if she could fix him some dinner. Fred still hadn't answered. He was grinning at Howard. "Hey, Howard . . . come here a minute." He reached out and poked a finger into Howard's stomach. "Putting on a little weight there, aren't we, old buddy?" Fred laughed. Charlotte asked if he was sure she couldn't fix him some dinner. "No, seriously," Fred said. Clasping his hands behind his neck, he went high on his toes, arching his chest. "No, seriously, nothing. I had to be up in New Haven this afternoon, and I just thought I'd drop by on the way back." He turned to the screen door again and looked out at the Pepsi machine. "Having . . . no *idea* . . . what I might . . . find . . ." He began to chuckle. "It's very nice, though, it really is."

"How about a drink, Fred?" Charlotte asked.

Fred put up his right hand as if he were a cop about to change the flow of traffic. "Can't stay more than a very few minutes, honey, gotta get home." His voice became crisp and matter-of-fact. "Gotta get home to New Jersey. Just stopped by for a second. Just wanted to see how you were . . . Hey, Howard . . ."

"What?"

Fred was looking at Howard with a fixed grin. Suddenly he exploded with laughter. "I don't mean to laugh," he said.

"We can tell," Charlotte said.

"I'll take the ice box," Fred said. "How much do you want for it?"

Charlotte laughed. "We came home from the tennis court this afternoon, and there they were. Already delivered."

"I don't get it," Fred said.

"Neither do we," Charlotte said.

"You mean—somebody had them delivered here?"

"Apparently," Charlotte said.

"Well, my God! How will you ever get rid of them?"

"Ace Haul," Howard said.

"Well . . ." Fred now made a transition. "Gotta get going. Before I go, I'd like to make one final pitch. Look, is it going to hurt you? Just one lousy night? It sounds like you're trying to prove something, that's what it sounds like to me.

How about it, Charlottesville?"

"Howard's the boss," Charlotte said.

"Sorry," Howard said. "I'm not coming."

Fred raised his eyebrows and spread his hands. "Okay, that's what I expected you to say."

"Sure you won't have a drink, Fred?" Charlotte asked.

"No thanks, sweetie, I can't. I gotta head out for Joisey. Right now." Fred's hand was on the knob of the screen door. "Hey, Howard . . ." He turned. "Marcia thinks this jacket's a little big for me. Do you?"

Howard nodded. "Yes," he said, "it hangs on you like a tent. It's a good looking jacket. It's a shame it doesn't fit you."

Fred scowled, grinned, and then scowled again. "I paid two hundred fifty dollars for the damned thing."

"How much?" Howard asked.

"Two-fifty." Fred tapped Howard just above the belt. "Get it off, get it off," he said. To Charlotte, he said, "Night, sweetie."

Howard followed him out. Fred paused at the refrigerator, sticking his head inside and sniffing. "I don't know who's been living in there," he said, "but whoever it was . . ." Fred started laughing again. Howard watched his face closely in the fading light. "Hey," he said.

Fred turned. "What?"

"Esquire!"

"Esquire?" Fred looked puzzled. "What are you saying *Esquire* for?"

Howard was watching the corners of Fred's mouth. "Because you're a lawyer," he said.

Fred's car was a six-months-old Cadillac. He opened the door and got in. "Listen, Howard," he said, "in all seriousness, what's behind all this? Why aren't you willing to come to the show? The show itself, hell, it's not all that important. Come on, level with me. Let's get it out in the open."

"Get what out in the open?"

"Let's for God's sake be honest."

Howard smiled. "Okay, well . . . it *is* a long way to drive, that's one thing."

"What else?"

"Well . . . I squirm."

"You—what?"

"I sit there in the audience and I squirm. I'm embarrassed for you. I don't think you sing as well as *you* think you sing. Sometimes you sound off-key. And when you act, you're always popping your eyes and there's a phoney grin you always use . . ."

Fred started the engine with a roar, then let it idle down. "Are you serious? Or are you just kidding?"

"I'm serious. But—if you get pleasure out of it, I think you should go right ahead."

Fred had both hands on the steering wheel, staring straight ahead. He stabbed the accelerator. The motor roared.

Casually, Howard leaned forward and spat on the hood of Fred's Cadillac.

"Hey!" Fred stuck his head from the window. "What the hell are you spitting on my car for?"

"I just felt like it," Howard said. "It'll dry." He stepped back to the driver's window. "No, that's not quite honest. The real reason is because you're the one responsible for all this damned junk in our yard, you bastard."

"Me?" Fred's voice wavered between indignation and laughter.

"Also the Esquire Dating Service."

"*Me?*" Fred was still trying not to laugh.

"Because I wouldn't come to your lousy show—I guess. My God! couldn't you have been content with one or the other?"

"O-*kay* . . . o-*kay* . . . what are you so mad about? Frankly I thought it was pretty damned funny."

"Yes," Howard said. "I guess it was." Gently he brought his hand down on the roof of the car. "It's costing me fifty bucks to get rid of this junk."

"Okay, so I'll send you a check."

"Was it worth it?"

"Every cent. Come on, Howard, what the hell's happening to you?" Fred held out his hand and Howard brushed his fingertips. "You're beginning to bug me," Fred said. He gave the accelerator another stab and put the car in reverse.

Howard stood watching. Fred backed the car around and as he headed out his voice swelled in sardonic song.

"*Some en-chant-ed eve-ning,*" he sang, blasted his horn twice and was gone.

Charlotte had been standing in the doorway and had heard every word. Just when he had thought she was under-reacting, as June would have expressed it, she now seemed to melt with joy.

"Howard!" She opened the screen door for him and threw her arms about his neck. "You really *are*—aren't you?"

"The supercilious bastard," Howard muttered.

He was discovering something which, although it hardly should have been surprising, nonetheless came to him as a surprise. So self-absorbed had he been all these years that he had gone along thinking that he was the only bastard around. It was fascinating, and strengthening, to find so many others.

He and Charlotte were scheduled to appear at a neighborhood cocktail party on Sunday evening. For a variety of reasons, Howard decided that he didn't want to go, and Charlotte went alone.

She was gone longer that he might have expected. Howard

read the Sunday paper for a while and then began to drink, at first in the kitchen and then out on the terrace. When it was dark he decided that he was hungry and he went inside and heated a can of soup. By then he had had several martinis. As he ate the soup, he paused occasionally and held the soup spoon close to the tip of his nose and looked at it cross-eyed.

He decided that he'd like some more soup and then thought it would be enjoyable to read while he ate. Looking about, he found an old magazine in Charlotte's studio and read of a young hominid called Leroy who died and fell into a lake. Almost two million years later, far down in an African gorge, in one of the very bottom layers, buried deep in time, his skull fossils had been found and pieced together with painstaking effort and skill.

With a feeling of great compassion, Howard pictured Leroy on the shores of the lake, cowering in the darkness in the cold pre-dawn of history, gnawing on bones.

He held his soup spoon to the tip of his nose again.

"Howard! Stop doing that!" Charlotte had returned. "You'll ruin your eyes. They're already giving you trouble. That man you showed the house to, Mr. Marble, Jimmy Marble . . . I heard at the party that he bought that horrible old Williston place near Ridgefield for one hundred seventy-five thousand dollars. It's a mausoleum . . . I drank too much, Howard. I'm going straight up to bed."

After she had gone upstairs, Howard went out to the meadow and walked about, mostly in a series of long, meandering arcs, thinking briefly about Marble but principally about Sadie. Convinced that he was now sober, he returned to the house. It was by then nearly 9:00.

In the darkness of the den, he deliberated a few minutes, then went upstairs and found Charlotte fast asleep. Back down in the den, he called Barney's Tavern and asked for Sadie. When she came on, she sounded out of breath.

"Sadie . . ."

"Yes, I'm fine. Are you?" He was speaking in a drone,
"Howard! Are you all *right*?"
keeping one ear trained toward the bedroom.

"I can hardly hear you," Sadie said. "Can you speak any
louder, Howard?"

"Is this any better?"

"Not much. Oh, Howard, I've been so worried."

"I'm sorry," he said. "If there'd been any way at all . . ."

"Oh, of course," she said. "Can you tell me where you
are?"

"I would if I could, you know that."

"Of course. I understand . . . what day is it there?"

Howard paused. "What day is it there?" he countered.
"Sunday?"

"Yes, Sunday night. Oh, Howard, I feel so relieved. I knew
that if you'd been anywhere in the country you'd have called
me, but I still worried terribly . . . This is a funny connection. I know you're far far away, yet it seems so clear—and
yet I can't hear you very well. Oh, Howard, I've missed you
so."

"I've missed you, Sadie . . ." Howard frowned. He
thought he had heard something upstairs.

"This is very considerate of you to call me," Sadie said,
"spending all this money."

Howard was listening intently.

"Howard . . . Howard, are you all right?"

With the phone cord stretched to its full length, Howard
was leaning toward the doorway, straining his ears.

"Howard . . . has something *happened*?"

"Sadie," he said in barely more than a whisper. "I think
somebody may be listening. I'm okay, I'm fine, but I'd better
hang up now. Good night, Sadie."

Silently he replaced the phone and for a few minutes sat

frozen in the darkness, listening, but there was no further sound from upstairs, and when he went up to the bedroom Charlotte was breathing evenly, the sheet pulled up to her chin.

Howard fell into bed stupefied. When he awoke the next morning, he felt more guilty about Sadie than ever. He felt lousy when he could lie to her and lousy when he couldn't. She was a very special case.

That day, however, his confidence returned, particularly when he thought about the way he had handled Fred. In late afternoon, just before it was time to leave, he discussed it with June. "Actually," he said, "a strange thing has happened. I don't think of truth and honesty as a game any more. I don't need any more pep talks, I don't think in terms of letting it all hang out. Usually I tell the truth because I'm too damned mad not to. And do you know something else?"

June was smiling. "What else?"

"If you went up tomorrow morning and told Personnel I wouldn't give a damn."

"Beautiful." June looked ecstatic. "That's exactly the way I knew it would happen. The Group was talking about that very thing the other night. The game—withers away, and you're left with something much more vital. You become your own man. Kevin said he had exactly the same experience."

"The hell with Kevin," Howard said.

June laughed.

They rode down on the elevator together and Howard, as he occasionally had in the past, asked if she'd like to share a cab with him to Grand Central and then keep it. In the lobby, while June waited for him near the revolving door, Howard veered off for some cigarettes. As he approached the newsstand, Malcolm Lorimer was just turning away, folding the evening paper and thrusting it under his arm. "Hiya," Howard said in the breezy tone he used with Lorimer.

"Howard . . ." Lorimer gave him an affectionate smile. He was aglow with suntan and his white hair gleamed. He put his arm around Howard's shoulder, gave it a squeeze and a pat and was gone.

As always, special attention from Lorimer raised Howard's spirits, and he looked about the lobby to see who might have noticed the special way Lorimer had treated him.

June had gone on through the revolving door and was waiting for him at the curb. "It's easier, of course," she said, "to tell the truth to people you feel you've been wronged by, but even so I'd be willing to bet that right this very minute you're a far superior person to your brother."

Howard chuckled. "Maybe," he said modestly. By now he was feeling very good.

A cab was drawing to the curb, and as they got in, Howard apparently closed the door with greater force than necessary, although he was not aware of having done so.

The clue was in the reaction of the driver. "Easy on nuh doah, easy on nuh doah," he said, turning to glare at them. "Glass breaks, you know what I mean? It *breaks*."

June stiffened. "Glass," she said.

"Yeah, lady, glass. It breaks."

"Right," June said. "I'll make a note of that. Remember that, Mr. Carew. Glass. It breaks." June was angry. There were pink puffs beneath her eyes.

The driver lurched off, disgust evident in his shoulders and in the set of his head beneath its tiny leather cap.

Although in the old days Howard might have let it pass, he knew now that he wouldn't. He waited only until he had settled upon what he felt was the proper blend of sternness and compassion.

"Driver," he said. "I have something to say."

"Whuh's that?"

"When somebody slams your door, I think you have a perfect right to object, because, just as you say—glass breaks."

"Damn right it breaks, buddy, listen, do you know how much it costs to replace door glass, not to mention the time I'm laid up? See that sign on the window there, it says, 'please do not slam door, thank you.' That's what I'm sayin'."

"However," Howard went on, "I think when you object, you might do it in a more civilized way." He felt June's eyes upon him. She was smiling.

"Whuh?" The driver threw a quick glance over his shoulder and swerved in time to miss a double-parked car.

"All I'm saying—" Howard began.

"Look!" the driver jolted to a stop at a red light. He was jabbing a forefinger deep into his own chest. "I make my livin' with this hack, don't forget."

"Right," Howard said. "But I still say there were ways you could have conveyed your objection without snarling, that's my only point. You had a perfect right to object."

"Gee, thanks, big deal." The cab made a screeching turn into Park Avenue.

"You could have said, 'Would you mind not slamming the door so hard, since glass is breakable . . .' " Howard felt June's hand on his knee.

"Oh my God!" the driver lamented. "That's what I coulda *said!*"

"Right."

"I coulda said, 'Would you mind not slammin' the door so hard since glass, it breaks.' Oh my God!" Momentarily the driver inclined his head upward, as if raising his eyes to heaven. He kept shaking his head.

"It's not enough we gotta get mugged . . ."

A block from Grand Central, Howard turned to June and asked, "Are you sure you want to keep it?"

"I'll get out and take another one," she said. "He might mug me." She patted his hand. Her eyes were shining.

The driver lurched up to the entrance, slammed to a stop and jerked down the flag. "Two-fifteen," he growled.

Howard handed up three singles. "You can keep the change," he said.

The driver glared at him as he helped June out. "Don't do me no favors," he said.

"I hope you have a pleasant evening," Howard said.

Muttering something about John Lindsay, the driver careened off.

Howard grinned. "Here's one," he said as another cab swung up. "Here, June . . ." He offered her some bills, but she refused. He helped her in and as the cab drove off she kissed the tips of her fingers.

As he turned away, Howard felt just fine. As he trotted down the stairway that led to the concourse, he kept smiling. Once on the concourse, he moved with the flow of the crowd to the gate, passed through and took the escalator down to the track level, where he started to walk briskly abreast of the train, in search of an unfilled coach.

Behind him he heard footsteps, the sound of running, and then a hand was touching his arm. "Howard . . . !"

He turned and came to a full, jolting halt. His ears went up in flames.

✳ fifteen

What he saw, what stood there facing him, was an apparition, with heavy gold hoops dangling from the ears, an apparition in a black laced bodice, sucked in at the slim waist, and the shortest of short white skirts, and sandals with thongs that wound about the calf. An apparition with long blonde hair and pale lips, parted now in disbelief. The apparition was staring at him as if he too were an apparition—staring from dark blue eyes rimmed with black makeup.

All in a split second he felt an overpowering sense of *déjà vu*. It was exactly like a recurring nightmare he had been having for months. In the nightmare he was always hurrying to the commuter train, bound for Connecticut, when suddenly he bumped into Sadie. She always stared at him with disbelief. "Howard!" she would say. "What are *you* doing here?"

"Howard!" Still clutching his arm, Sadie was staring at him. "What are *you* doing here?"

His impulse was to bolt, to run like hell, to hide under the train and refuse to come out. He wanted to say no, he was not Howard, whoever Howard was; that instead he was a Connecticut burgher named, say, Philip, who was hurrying home to his wife and family. In one nightmare he had said, "Sorry, there must be some mistake."

Now, with a grin unbecomingly sheepish for one who trafficked in international peril, one who so recently had been hanging about the Berlin Wall, he said: "Hi."

"Oh, God," Sadie said, "I just can't believe it. Oh, *How-*

ard!" She clutched his arm with both hands and held it to her bosom. Howard's eyes began to dart. "I just don't understand. How did you *get* here—on this *very* train?"

Since they were still on the platform, he was, of course, not yet on this train nor any other train. Yet there was no other train he could say he was headed for, unless he pointed to one four tracks away, the boarding of which would have involved jumping from the platform six feet down to the track-bed and even then, even after scrambling across the tracks, he would end up on the train's blind side, its unboardable façade—unless he wriggled on his stomach beneath a coupling.

Barely moving his lips, not looking her in the eye, he muttered, "Boston."

"Boston? This is the Westport train. You mean it goes on to Boston? Oh yes, of course . . . I guess it would. Naturally. Well, come *on* then. Let's get a seat." Linking her arm through his, she started striding ahead. Howard permitted himself to be tugged. "Oh, Howard, I love you. I just can't believe it—it's like a dream."

"You're right."

After a few yards, he withdrew his arm from hers, as if to indicate that he needed two free hands to hold what he happened to be holding. Then he realized that what he happened to be holding, supporting with both hands, was his commuter ticket book. Quickly he stuffed it into his pocket.

"What's that you have, Howard?"

"My papers," Howard said.

Among the many things he now wished was that her skirt were six inches longer—even three inches longer would help; and that the black bodice were laced a little tighter—or a lot less tight, rather. All the while his eyes were darting sidelong, inspecting each coach for familiar faces.

Sadie paused. "Here?"

"No, let's keep going."

"Howard, how did you *get* here? Did you know last night?"

He shook his head. "They never tell us anything."

"You poor man, you must be exhausted. When did you land?"

"A little after three."

"At Kennedy? And then what, took a cab here?"

"Car brought me," he said from the side of his mouth.

His brain was racing this way and that, darting and veering and bumping into things. He was walking very rapidly. She ran a few steps to catch up with him. "How about this one, Howard?"

"Let's try a few more," he suggested.

"Gosh, if we don't stop walking soon we'll be in Connecticut," she said. "Isn't that the locomotive up there?"

"Okay, here," Howard said. "We should be able to get a seat on this one, I think."

"I should think," Sadie said. "It's totally empty."

She stepped aboard. Looking over his shoulder down the enormous length of the platform, he followed. As she walked ahead of him up the aisle, she turned abruptly and threw her arms about him. "Howard, is it you? Are you here?"

For a few seconds he was distracted by the sheer pleasure of being with her. He kissed her, she clung to him, and then he led her to a seat, placing her next to the window and sinking into place beside her, comforted somewhat by the sheer emptiness of the coach.

"Is this safe for you, Howard?" She linked her arm through his and raised his hand to her bare knee.

"Yes, this should be fine."

"You seem worried. Is somebody following you?"

"I don't think so. Not so far as I know." He glanced at

his watch. Only three minutes before departure. Once the train was underway he would be able to think clearly. Up until now he had been operating on raw instinct. "What are *you* doing on this train?" he asked. The question had an edgy undertone of accusation. "Did you get the part?"

"No," she said, "I'm watching the show tonight and talking to the director later. I did a reading on Saturday and they told me I had to work on my projection. I don't really think they want me."

"You mean—you were out here—Saturday?"

"Yes, Saturday evening. Why?"

"Nothing." Two minutes.

"Where were you? I'm sorry, I shouldn't ask."

Howard pressed her hand. One minute. An elderly couple came up the aisle and sat a few seats ahead. And then in a matter of seconds there was an abrupt stream of passengers, overflowing from the coaches to the rear. No one that he knew.

Thank God.

"Gosh, Howard, this train is really crowded. These must be commuters going home to Connecticut. This must be the commuting hour."

"Yes," Howard said. "I think it is."

He looked at his watch. Sadie kept talking. She laughed at something she had been telling him about her agent, or possibly the director. Having no idea what she was talking about, Howard answered with a full-throated chuckle. He was feeling a little better.

Looking at his watch again, he heard the trainman call, "All aboard!" in the special dialect trainmen used for the phrase, and it sounded beautiful. Howard found himself relaxing. He pressed her hand, nuzzled her knee with his knuckles. She pressed his hand to her cheek.

The train lurched into motion and then, lurching up the aisle, came a final passenger.

Howard had hated Mark Patterson for years. Not until now did he realize how deeply that hatred went. Feeling a hand on his shoulder, he looked up into the eyes of Mark Patterson. "Good evening," Patterson said with a smirk.

"Right," Howard replied, feeling his ears burn.

Harrison passed on but not far enough by a long shot. Glancing over his shoulder for a quick, raised-eyebrow inspection tour of Sadie, he found the refuge he was seeking only two seats in front of them, on the same side of the aisle. The intervening seat was empty. Folding his seersucker jacket, he placed it on the overhead rack and then slumped into his seat, resting his head against the window, as if prepared to spend the hour and a half or so in deep repose.

Howard discovered that with one hand he was putting a tight grip on two fingers of the other.

"He knows you?" Sadie asked.

"He may *think* he does." Howard was looking grim.

"I understand." Sadie grasped his hand. "Is he—tailing you?"

"I don't think so," he muttered. "I'll know—by where he gets off the train."

Howard's voice was a deep drone. He was barely moving his lips.

With Sadie, however, it was a different matter, and Howard was wondering how in God's name the director could ever have found fault with her projection. There was something about the theater. She had been trained to speak it so they could *hear* it—all the way up in the second balcony—without ever seeming to shout. She had explained this to him once. It had to do with articulation, something about the way the words were formed with the lips and muscular control of the diaphragm.

"I hate to think of you going all the way to Boston," she said, addressing the second balcony.

Howard winced and closed his eyes.

"Do you feel the time-change?"

Howard opened his eyes in time to see Patterson twist in his seat.

"Not too much," he muttered.

"What time did you leave this morning—your time?"

Patterson was twisting this way and that. He couldn't seem to get comfortable.

"That man bothers you, doesn't he?" Sadie kissed his hand. "Are you carrying your gun, Howard?"

Howard's head wobbled. Looking Sadie in the eye, he put his finger to his lips. She nodded. He looked over his shoulder at the conductor, who was coming up the aisle, collecting tickets.

Reaching into the inside pocket of his jacket for something to write on, Howard pulled out his commuter ticket book and quickly shoved it back. Reaching again, he came up with the gas bill. "Do you have something to write on?" he asked. Sadie pulled an envelope from her purse. Supporting it with his knee, Howard printed in large letters: BOSTON.

Sadie looked puzzled. "Why are you—oh, of course. I understand." She glared in the direction of Patterson.

The conductor was at Howard's elbow. Sadie handed her ticket across and Howard showed the conductor what he had printed, reaching at the same time for his billfold. The conductor looked at Howard with sympathy. "That'll be seventeen eighty, please." Howard gave him a twenty and received his change. When the conductor had passed along, he did some more printing, holding it up for Sadie to see:

I CAN'T TALK ABOUT MY MOVEMENTS. OKAY?

"Oh, of course." Sadie looked contrite. "I'm sorry, darling."

"Thanks," he whispered.

"What, Howard?"

"I said thanks."

"Oh." She smiled. "I love you."

He patted her leg.

"It's all right to say 'I love you,' isn't it?"

Howard's eyes were fixed on the back of Patterson's abominable head. His brain began to work. "Well . . ." he said in a loud voice, "almost to Greenwich"—although they were in fact still a good distance from Greenwich. "Do you know much about Greenwich?"

Sadie looked puzzled. "Me?"

"I've always been interested in Greenwich, for some reason," Howard said. "Did you know that Greenwich was settled in 1614, as part of New Amsterdam?"

Sadie was admiring him with her eyes. The people across the aisle were looking at him with interest. "Gosh, Howard," Sadie said. "How did you know that?"

The reason he knew it was because he had once run an article on Greenwich in *The Electron.*

"I don't know," he said, "I just happened to remember it. Greenwich consists of nine self-contained sections and occupies about fifty square miles of gently rolling land, rising from sea level to an elevation approximating the height of the Washington Monument."

Sadie shook her head. "It always amazes me how much you remember. Your memory is fantastic."

"On the Old Post Road is an inn where Israel Putnam was surprised by the British and escaped by riding his horse down a steep flight of stone steps."

"What's this?" Sadie asked as the train lost speed.

"It's only Greenwich," Howard said miserably.

When the train started again, ending the dead silence which had prevailed during the station stop at Greenwich, he plunged ahead. "How is your father?" he asked in a voice loud enough to be heard easily by Patterson.

"My father?"

Howard realized immediately that the question was a mistake.

"He's fine," Sadie said. "I called home a couple of nights ago and told him how you felt about being investigated."

Howard twitched. "Excuse me a minute," he said, heading back to the lavatory for a good cry.

In the cubicle, with the door securely locked behind him, he confronted himself in the mirror. His head was wobbling and he was moving his shoulders unnecessarily. He closed his eyes to shut out the sight of his face, then opened them and gave himself a grin of sheer tormented idiocy. I'm in here, he promised his reflection, and I'm not coming out for days and days. Maybe never. I like it in here. I love it in here.

The train was losing speed for Stamford.

Resolutely he jerked open the door. As he strode up the aisle, he gave Patterson a steely glance of contempt—a glance that was totally lost on Patterson since it was directed at the back of his head. Sadie patted the seat.

"Are you all right?" she asked, as the train drifted to a halt.

"I'm fine," he said. "I couldn't get the door unlocked. American trains are really lousy, compared to European trains."

"I've been sitting here wondering, Howard . . . why you didn't fly straight to Boston from Kennedy."

Howard closed his eyes. "Well . . . the trick is always to do the unexpected," he muttered. "Always do what seems, you know—least logical."

"I understand. Oh, yes, I can see that, of course."

"I was just thinking about Israel Putnam."

"You mean in the bathroom just now?"

"What?"

"I say, in the bathroom just now . . . you were thinking of Israel Putnam?"

"I was thinking what a tremendously difficult thing it would be to bring off—riding a horse down a steep flight of steps."

"God, yes!"

"He deserves a lot of credit," Howard went on. "Men were a lot tougher back in those days."

"Nobody could be much tougher than you are, Howard."

Patterson by now had given up all semblance of repose and was sitting erect, giving an impression of total alertness. His head was moving in a way that a head might move if the shoulders beneath it happened to be shaking with mirth.

"Maybe so," Howard said, "but I've never tried doing that."

"What?"

"Riding a horse down a flight of steps."

"How many people have?" Sadie took his hand. "I'm worried, Howard. I don't feel close to you. There's something different about you. Am I turning you off? Is it something you can tell me?"

"I hate to . . ." Howard hung his head. "Because it sounds so full of self-pity." She placed his hand on her knee again. "But the fact is that I'm absolutely groggy, absolutely out on my feet. I haven't slept in—four days."

"Howard! Oh, you poor man!"

"I'll be fine," he said. "I'm getting a little bit concerned though . . . about . . ." He inclined his head toward Patterson.

"Him?"

Howard nodded. His voice dropped to a whisper. "Maybe the safest thing would be to pretend that I'm just a plain commuter, going home on the commuter train, okay?"

"Good." Sadie looked happy. "All right. And that I am too, okay?"

"Right." Howard patted her leg.

In a loud voice, Sadie said, "Did you remember to pay the milk bill, Howard?"

It wasn't exactly what he had had in mind. "As a matter of fact," he said, "maybe I'd just better sit here with my eyes closed. I should try to rest a little, I may have a big night ahead."

"Please do, Howard. Don't mind me."

"Maybe I should."

"Here . . . let me get my arm around you, and you can put your head on my shoulder, okay?"

Howard sat up straight. "I can't do it," he said. "I just refuse to waste time sleeping when I can be with you—no matter *how* tired I am."

"Oh, Howard . . ."

He looked through the window, searching through the evening light for the Westport depot.

"Darien, Darien . . ."

The quarter-miles clicked slowly by.

"Westport . . . Westport . . . next stop, Westport . . ."

The conductor was slurring it from the rear of the coach . . . but Howard knew what he was saying. "I guess this is where you get off, Sadie . . . How long do you expect to stay?"

"Out here? I'm going back tonight."

"Oh." Howard nodded, his eyes on Patterson. "Well, I have no idea how long I'll be gone this time . . . but I'll call you just as soon as I get to New York . . ."

171

"Please do, Howard. How about Los Angeles? Are we still going?"

"Of course," he said. "I'm living for it."

"Me too." Picking up his hand again, she touched it to her lips and then pressed it hard against her leg. "I don't want to leave you." She squirmed closer, looking into his eyes, lips parted.

"This was a bonanza, Sadie. So totally unexpected. A marvelous surprise."

Patterson was on his feet, standing in the aisle, pulling his jacket down from the rack. He was looking straight at Howard.

"Look!" Sadie said. "That man's getting off. That relieves my mind."

Howard shrugged. "I wasn't really worried about him."

As Sadie leaned close, the train lurched and he bumped his nose against one of the large gold hoops. She laughed. He stood in the aisle, letting her out. "Bye, darling," she said and moved on up the aisle, giving Patterson a venomous glance as she passed.

Patterson in turn was looking with surprise at Howard, seeing that he was making no move to get off the train. Having all these years grinned expectantly at the mere sight of Howard, Patterson, from the look in his eye, now seemed to feel that Howard had lived up to his expectations and more. Shaking his head, he followed Sadie up the aisle.

When they had gone, Howard collapsed in his seat. He looked from the window to see Sadie waving from the platform and calling something. He cupped his hand to his ear. It sounded as though she were saying, "Please be careful."

With a final wave, she disappeared. Again Howard collapsed and again turned. Standing on the platform, just beneath the window, Patterson placed his hands on his hips.

In his owlish eyes there was a look of vast enjoyment. With an impish wave, he turned away, shaking his head.

A few miles beyond Westport lay the town of Fairfield. It was here that Howard left the train that evening. After a considerable wait, he commandeered a taxi which, for a stiff fee, carried him back down the Connecticut Turnpike to Westport, dropping him at the depot where he walked to the parking lot and got into his car.

By then the reaction had set in and as he drove home he felt miserable.

At dinner he ate little and talked less. He kept looking at Charlotte, as if sizing her up, and finally she noticed. "Howard . . . what's wrong? Is anything wrong?" He kept shaking his head, telling her no, there was nothing wrong.

They were having their coffee when Howard, in reaching for one of the candles to light his cigarette, brushed his coffee spoon with his arm. The spoon fell to the floor and bounced. Unable to reach it, he slipped from his chair and went under the table after it. With the spoon in hand, he started to back out on his hands and knees, but instead he slid forward and lay on his stomach, cradling his head with one arm.

For a few seconds there was silence. Then Charlotte said, "Howard . . ."

"Yes?"

"Are you all right?"

"Yes."

"Where are you?"

"Right here. Under the table."

"What are you doing?"

"Nothing."

From above there was a puzzled laugh. She had slipped off her loafers. He watched one of her feet come to rest on top of

173

the other. Her big toe wiggled. "Howard . . . are you really all right?"

"Yes, I'm fine."

Charlotte's feet moved. She was getting up, going to the kitchen, making small clattering noises, pouring a cup of coffee, he judged. Then she was back again, her bare feet planted side by side, and he could hear the faint sound of sipping.

Howard by now was lying flat on his back, hands clasped behind his head, looking up at the underside of the table. There was a sticker which said C-23, an identification sticker put there by the moving company when they had moved to Connecticut.

"Howard, aren't you ever coming back up and sit at the table?"

"Yes, of course."

"Well—when?"

Howard took a deep breath, He flipped over and lay on his stomach again, resting his cheek against his arm. Once more her feet were at eye-level.

"Not until I've told you something," he said.

Her toes began to wriggle.

"What is it you want to tell me?"

Howard took another deep breath. "Marriage is a strange institution, wouldn't you say?"

Her feet were now in repose. "Yes, I suppose it is."

"It places some strange restrictions on people, I do know that much. I mean—on people who happen to be married. Of course all I'm speaking of is the American version of marriage —because that, of course, is all I know . . ."

He stared hard at her loafers. They were stiff, shiny, almost new. He was glad she had bought them. If at that moment he had been staring at her *old* loafers, so sad and pitiable, with scuff marks at the toes and a hole in the sole, he would have been stopped dead in his tracks. He could not have gone on.

"In other countries, of course," he was saying, "there are other versions of marriage. It's very strange to think of morality being an accident of geography, isn't it?" He offered an ironic chuckle.

Above there was silence.

"Charlotte . . ."

"Yes?"

"What are you doing?"

"I'm sitting here listening to you." One bare foot was tapping gently against the rug.

"Oh. Okay. Hey, guess what?"

"What, Howard?"

"There's a wad of chewing gum stuck up under the table."

"Is there?"

"Yes. I wonder who did it. I wonder how long it's been here."

She didn't answer. Instead her legs swung aside and her face appeared.

"What are you doing?" Howard asked with a frown.

"I'm just looking to see what *you're* doing."

"Stay up there. I'm coming up in a minute." Her face disappeared, and her feet rested on the floor once more. "I'm only staying down here because it's comfortable," he said.

Silence.

"Okay?" he called.

"Yes, Howard, okay." Her voice now had a distinct edge which he couldn't identify. "Howard . . ."

"Yes?"

"Are you sure you're all right?"

"Yes."

"Are you trying to tell me something?"

He hesitated. "Yes . . ."

"Is it something you've been afraid to tell me?"

"Yes."

"Are you trying to tell me you're having an affair?"
"Yes!—how did you know?"

So great was his relief that it came out as a shout of grati-
tude. Then he realized how his voice must have sounded.
"Yes, I'm afraid I am," he said, and his tone now was subdued,
contrite. He lay there bracing himself for whatever might
come.

He saw her feet rise a few inches off the floor and then go
back down again, resting now only on the heels, with the rest
of each foot angled upward. Her feet began to pivot on the
heels. The pivoting became more rapid. Her feet were doing
a sort of dance, and he watched curiously.

Her feet came to rest. She was slipping on her loafers and
now she was up from the table, striding from the room.

"Charlotte! Where are you going?"

"Out," she called back. "I'd like to drive around for a
while."

The screen door closed behind her.

Within ten minutes she telephoned him. "Howard . . . I
won't be back tonight. I may be gone for a couple of days,
but I'll be in touch with you, okay?"

"Charlotte! Listen now, we can work this out. I don't want
you to do anything crazy. All we—"

"Howard!" She interrupted him. "Just a minute. Let me
tell you . . . Don't worry about me, I'll be okay. And I
promise I won't do anything crazy. So go to sleep and get
some rest. Good night."

She hung up.

✳ sixteen

Howard stayed home from the office the next day, waiting for Charlotte to call.

It was the first day of September, and the weather wavered between summer and fall. In the morning the air was crisp and autumnal but there was a gentle south wind which brought a warm afternoon. The meadow was still a thick green tangle but around its borders a few trees had begun to show spots of color.

As Charlotte had said, autumn was a time of transition.

Howard tramped over the meadow, picking up beer cans; he spent an hour in her studio, looking at her old canvases; he sat on the terrace, reading the newspaper. At some point he found that he had dropped the newspaper to the ground and was staring endlessly at a single leaf that fluttered and danced at the end of a branch. Watching it made him feel calm.

All day long the phone was silent.

By late afternoon he had made a decision. He had to end it with Sadie, and tell her all. There was no other way he could live with himself.

Toward evening he left the house for New York. Instead of taking the train, he drove and on the way he rehearsed the way he would tell her. He drove more slowly than was his custom and occasionally he spoke his lines aloud. "I'm nobody, Sadie," he muttered as he passed the cutoff to the Tappan Zee Bridge. "I've never been to Afghanistan or the Berlin Wall, in fact I've never been much of anywhere. I'm just a slob who runs a magazine and rides back and forth on the commuter train. I've got a wife, a house in Connecticut, two cars, two lawn mowers and a hairpiece."

When he got to New York he put his car in a public garage, walked two blocks to Barney's Tavern and took a seat at the bar. "The same, Mr. Jefferson?" George already had a glass in his hand, and he had asked the question with his usual deference.

"Yes, George, thanks. The same." Howard looked at his reflection in the dark mirror. George was mixing the martini and now saying, "You looking for Sadie, Mr. Jefferson? I don't think she's working tonight. Hey—Peggy!" He called to one of the waitresses. "Sadie working tonight?"

Peggy didn't break stride. "She's off tonight," she called back.

Howard nodded. "I'll drink it anyway, George."

When George placed the martini before him, he took a sip and then went back to call Sadie from the telephone booth next to the men's room.

"Howard! You're back? Already?"

"Yep. I'm coming up. Okay?"

"Are you all right? You sound—low."

"I'll be up."

"*Hurry!*"

Returning to the bar, he sipped the martini slowly while George busied himself behind the bar. As always, George was paying respect to his silence. George never said anything until he got a signal of some kind.

Howard took a deep breath and let it go. George looked at him sympathetically. "Tough day, huh?"

Howard nodded. "Yep."

"I guess in your line of work, Mr. Jefferson, all days are tough in one way or another, huh?"

Smiling, Howard picked up his glass and drained it. He

shook his head when George asked if he wanted another one. Pulling a five dollar bill from his wallet, he laid it on the bar. "Keep it, George," he said.

"Say! Thanks, Mr. Jefferson."

"You're more than welcome, George," Howard said, and then he just sat there for a while, thinking that this very probably would be the last time he would ever set foot in Barney's Tavern. Thinking this, he felt a lump in his throat. He looked toward the rear, seeing the ghost of Sadie, picking her way through the maze of tables, looking intent and harried, except when she looked out toward the bar and smiled at him.

The lump in his throat was worse. He sat there, looking at his hands and looking into the mirror. George was opening a bottle of onions.

Presently Howard said, "George, speaking of my line of work—what do you think it is? What do you think I do for a living?"

George grinned. "Well, I've made a lot of guesses."

"I think maybe I should tell you," Howard said.

George shook his head. "It's none of my business, Mr. Jefferson. Look, I know it's a rotten world, and I know somebody's gotta do the dirty work but exactly who's doing what, that's none of my business, know what I mean? My wife, she always tells me some people like danger, they really enjoy it, you know? I never liked it much myself . . ." George was polishing glasses. "At night I go to sleep telling myself, 'George, you're a lucky guy. Here you are in bed at night in a lousy city and yet all around the city and all around the country for that matter, and the world too, as far as that goes, people doing the dirty work for you—people arresting hoods and tracking down thieves and intercepting drug shipments and seeing to it that foreign agents don't get away with too much.'" George spread his hands. "So I say to myself, 'George, you're a lucky guy.'"

As Howard made his way to the door, George called, "So long, Mr. Jefferson. Take care now."

Howard found a parking space just across the street from Sadie's building. As he got out and slammed the door, he found himself from years of habit darting covert glances up and down the block. But on this night he felt no thrill of adventure, no sense of being a cat burglar, no sense of making a frontal assault on the Himalayas, nor of sailing a small boat around the world. He felt plain lousy.

Sadie met him at the door in her pale blue nightgown with the white ribbons. Her hair was caught in back with a strip of blue velvet. The pinup lamp was on, she had been reading in bed. While he took off his shoes she pulled the ribbon off and shook her hair loose. "Hurry, Howard . . ." She was in bed now, turning off the lamp. "Howard . . . I'm in a great big double hammock and it's a summer night and I'm lying there, looking up at the stars, waiting for you to come out of the house. It's our hammock and our yard and our nice little house, and you have a safe plain job and my name is Sadie Jefferson and every day you go back and forth on the train—"

Howard moaned.

"Howard, what's wrong? It's all right, darling, don't worry about it. Please. It's perfectly all right, it really is. I know that you love me. Here. Just lie on my arm."

With a heavy sigh, Howard reached for a cigarette. With its glowing tip, he traced the curve of the shadow on the ceiling. Sadie lay quietly beside him.

Howard kept smoking and tracing the shadow and finally he heard his own voice. "Sadie, I'm not going to be able to see you anymore."

At first he thought she was asleep. In the faint crimson light, her eyes were closed. She didn't move.

"Sadie . . ."

"It was something I expected," she murmured. "I'm not too surprised. I shouldn't ask why. Should I?"

Howard let his head fall back on the pillow and closed his eyes. "I'm being transferred," he said.

"I understand," Sadie said.

"That's really—all I can tell you, Sadie."

"Don't try, Howard. I understand." She sighed and sat up. "Oh, gosh . . ."

"Sadie . . ." His voice faltered.

"Don't feel sad about it, Howard. Listen . . ." She was sitting above him, her head fell forward, and the ends of her long hair brushed his face. "If I could only make you understand . . . how much it's meant to me just to know you, and to know that you've loved me . . ."

Howard groaned. "You're going to make me bust out crying, please don't."

"I have to tell you this, Howard . . . no kidding, I really do. You've made me feel important—at a time when I needed so badly to feel important, a time when I wasn't getting anywhere, and it was so necessary for me to feel that I was something and somebody. It made me feel sort of in touch with the world, with an important part of the world. Don't you understand?"

Howard couldn't say anything.

"Gosh, up at Barney's, knowing how everybody felt about you up there . . . George and everybody, and the other waitresses. I'd be waiting on a table, and I'd look out toward the bar and see you sitting there and I'd think to myself— God! That's Howard Jefferson sitting at that bar and he likes me. *Me.* And I'd feel so good, just marvelous. Do you understand, Howard?"

"I guess so," Howard said miserably.

"It gave me so much joy and—confidence—to know that

you were who you were and what you were—even though I
didn't even really *know* who you were." She patted his head.
"Do you understand, Howard?"

"I'm beginning to, I guess."

She lay next to him again, burrowing into his shoulder.
"From now on, whenever I think of you I'll—think of you
the way I've *always* thought of you. Usually I think of you
on a plane, flying across the Atlantic and sometimes I'd see
you on the beach at the French Riviera . . . sometimes in a
small stark room above a store in East Berlin, living with some
sexy girl and I'd hate her. Sometimes I'd see you running
down a deserted street, late at night, sort of zigzagging over
wet cobblestones. Any time you shot your gun it never made
any noise. It always had a silencer on it. And whatever you
were doing, I always knew it was something decent and necessary and never cruel."

Howard now lay face-down. His voice was muffled by the
pillow. Sadie tugged at his shoulder, trying to turn him over
but he clung to the pillow. "Howard . . . please don't cry.
Please."

She kept stroking his head until finally he sat up straight
and reached for a cigarette. "Anyway," she said, "I don't feel
sorry for myself because I think maybe I'll make it on the
stage now, I have a strong feeling that I will."

Howard lay smoking and tracing while she told him about
her trip to the Westport Playhouse.

"Even though I didn't get the part, I could tell the director
really liked me," she said. "He's doing a play off Broadway
in October and he thinks I'll be perfect for the lead. He likes
me because he says I'm so trusting and naïve and guileless, he
thinks the public is ready for somebody like me. I didn't
know whether to be flattered or not. He made me sound so
old-fashioned and sort of wide-eyed and trustful."

"Be flattered, Sadie," Howard said. Reaching up, he turned

on the pinup lamp. Without eye makeup she looked very young. He stared at the rounded softness of her lower lip, at the delicacy of her chin. She looked fifteen. "Be flattered," he said again. "Don't change. Be this way forever." He kept staring at her face and then he moaned, "Oh, God," and turned away. He swung his feet to the floor and sat on the edge of the bed, looking at them. "Sadie . . ."

"Yes, Howard?"

"I'm going now." He put on his shoes and stood. Sadie circled the bed. He shook his head helplessly. "I—oh, my God . . ."

"We don't have to tell each other how much we've meant to each other, Howard. Don't try. There's no need."

He held her close, kissed her, pulled her head to his shoulder. "You can't tell me where you're going—not even that much?"

"Only that I'm being transferred . . ." Howard looked her in the eye. "Back to where I started out."

"Hmmmmmmm . . ." Sadie frowned. "That sounds like another country. I know I shouldn't try to guess, but—if you're from another country, why don't you speak with a foreign accent?"

Howard spread his hands. His tongue brought forth nothing.

"Do you hate the United States, Howard? Do you mean it harm?"

"No. I've never meant anybody any harm in my whole life, Sadie."

"Yes, I believe you, Howard."

"I think it's true," he said.

"Well . . ." Sadie was looking him in the eye, and there was something about her face that he had never seen before. He had paid so little regard to her career. Now, for no reason that was apparent, he was reminded that she was an actress.

She took a long strand of hair and placed it over one eye, looking at him with the other. "Now I think I know what you were, Howard. I think I've figured it out. You were one of those things, what are they called?—a double agent. Weren't you?"

Howard hung his head. He stood there smiling sadly at the floor. "Yeah, I guess you could say that . . ." He kissed her head, pulled open the door and walked out, closing it quickly behind him, not looking back.

✳ seventeen

Howard was dazed.

He had stopped at a toll booth on the Merritt Parkway and was handing the man a quarter and taking the nickel change . . .

He sat on his terrace, looking up at what he thought to be Cassiopeia's Chair, although it might have been Jacob's Gallows.

At six in the morning he stood at the kitchen sink eating his Grape Nuts, the spoon poised, empty. He was staring past it through the window, into the gray light.

He turned on the record player and filled the house with sound.

Charlotte called in mid-afternoon. "Howard . . ."

"Are you all right?"

"Yes, I'm fine," she said.

"Where are you?"

"It doesn't matter where I am."

"When are you coming back?"

"When I'm ready . . ."

"How can I reach you?"

"You can't. I'm going to please myself, Howard. You didn't hesitate to please yourself. Now it's my turn, old friend."

"This puts me in a strange position," he said. "But I guess I deserve it."

"You sure do. Well, I'll call you again, old friend."

"You can do me a favor, Charlotte."

"What's that?"

"Stop calling me 'old friend.' "

She laughed. "That's the way I think of you. Bye."

There was no word from her for three days but on the fourth evening when he returned home from work he found a note on the kitchen table. It said: "I came by to pick up some things. C."

Most of the dresses were gone from her closet and when he looked into her studio he found that she had taken her easel and brushes and quite a few of her canvases. The next morning he also realized that she had taken the electric coffee pot.

That morning on the way to work he entered the same mid-Manhattan barber shop he had patronized for almost twenty years. With no hesitation whatever he instructed his long-time barber to shorten his hair on top, to take some of the bushiness out of the sideburns—and to strip off his hairpiece and throw it away. "Don't scalp me," he said, "but give me a clean look around the ears."

"You say throw it away—the hairpiece?" his barber asked.

"Right."

"That's not gonna leave you with much."

"I'll have what I have," Howard said.

"What kinda Rhett Butler cut's that gonna be?"

"I don't care," Howard said.

"You're flying in the face of fashion." His barber brightened. "But it's okay with me, I'm going broke with the fashion."

While the barber was at work, Howard kept his nose buried in a magazine, deliberately averting his eyes. When the job was done, he looked at the face in the mirror and grunted. His hairline had receded noticeably just in the month or so since the hairpiece had last been shampooed, and it was far worse than he remembered it from the old pre-hairpiece days. A gap sliced far back into the side-part, and the effect was of half a part. My God, I'm ugly, he thought. Really ugly. My ears stick out. He looked sallow, understated, an aging Ivy League type in a slim black tie and a white button-down shirt. No mustache, no beard, no mutton-chops—a member of the Then Generation.

"Maybe half a Rhett Butler cut," the barber said.

Howard's eye was drawn, as most anybody's would be drawn, to the patch of very white skin which had been covered by the hairpiece. It made a fish-belly contrast with the rest of his face, which still had some tan from the summer.

"You like it?" his barber asked dubiously.

Resolutely Howard stepped from the chair. "It's what I asked for," he said, pulling on his jacket.

As he paid and tipped the barber, he glanced into the waste basket and saw his hairpiece. Well, he breathed, so long . . . old friend.

When he walked into the office a few minutes later, June was on the telephone. As she looked up, her eyes widened. Simultaneously she crossed her legs. For the past several days she had been wearing blouses and very short skirts instead of her zippered jump-suits. "Wow!" She formed the word with her lips.

Howard grinned and went on in to his desk.

"Okay, okay," he heard her saying into the phone. "Is that my fault? You say you want to live with the Hopi Indians, then for God's sake go *live* with the Hopi Indians. That doesn't mean that *I* have to go live with the Hopi Indians . . ."

Howard opened the morning mail and started throwing it at the trash basket.

"Wow!"

He looked up to find June in the doorway, staring at him with what seemed to be admiration. He grinned. "Ugly, huh?"

"No, not at all. It—it turns me off so much that it turns me on."

Howard laughed. "Did Mrs. Carew call?" He had told her about Sadie and Charlotte a few days earlier.

"No. Would you like some coffee?"

Howard said he would. While she was gone he kept throwing things at the trash basket. When she returned with the coffee, she took the chair next to his desk and carefully removed the lids from the two containers.

Sipping her coffee she asked, "Are you worried about your wife?"

"Yes."

"I'm sure she's fine. How do you feel about Sadie?"

"Lousy." He shoved his coffee aside to let it cool off.

"You've been living an illusion, Mr. Carew. No kidding. Not that illusions are wrong necessarily. We all need them. Illusions are a protective sheath. But sometimes they're the wrong ones, or they wear out."

"Maybe . . ."

"And as for Sadie—gosh, you don't need any little baby girl adoring you with her big blue eyes. It should be obvious to you why Sadie appealed to you so much. We've discussed it in the Group."

"I'd just as soon not hear about it," Howard said. Abruptly he gulped his coffee, burning his throat.

"Besides, you should stop thinking of women as nothing but sexual objects. Women are people. A woman and a man are simply reverse sides of the same coin—whose sexual organs happen to be conveniently placed . . ." June spread her hands. "Otherwise there's no difference . . . I never asked you—how do you feel about women's lib?"

Carefully Howard sipped his coffee. "Pretty much the way I feel about high heels for men," he said.

"I don't think you really mean that any more."

"Maybe not. Well . . . anyway . . ." Howard clapped his hands hard and then dusted his palms together. "I sure followed your advice. Icarus and camels and horses and wives —my God!"

June was smiling. "I'm not sure you've lost a thing that you really wanted. Just think about it for a while."

"That's what I've been doing," Howard said with bitterness. "I've been thinking about it for a while."

"What you've gained is far more valuable than what you've lost. You've gained your soul—I think."

"Mmmmmm." Howard frowned. "What does it profiteth a man to gain his soul . . . if in the prothess he loseth his wife, his mistress, his neighbors, his—"

"Hairpiece . . ."

"Yeah." Howard's hand moved to his head. It was a shock to feel only naked skin where hair once had been.

"You don't know for a fact that you've lost Mrs. Carew," June said. "She may be just playing for time, letting you sweat a little."

Howard sipped his coffee, making no reply.

"And—" June said, walking to the window. "If she *has* gone for good . . ." She turned with a smile.

"Yes?"

She had carried her coffee with her and was now smirking at him over the rim of the cup. There was something in her eyes that made him uncomfortable. "Yes?" he asked again.

"You could move in with me," she said.

Howard lit a cigarette, taking a good long time about it. "How about Hank?" he asked finally.

"I kicked him out about ten days ago. He's going off to live with the Indians."

"Well I'll be damned."

She was laughing at the expression on his face. "Look, I'm not talking about marriage, that's the last thing I want. But we could live together and see how it goes."

Howard dragged deeply on his cigarette, saying nothing.

"It might be fun," June said. "You can be a young middle-aged man in the process of finding yourself all over again, a man who's been given a second chance."

"That sounds like a protective sheath, June."

"Maybe so. But we could try it—see if it wears out."

Howard shook his head. "I'm not really sure I could ever make a physical commitment to you," he said deadpan.

June was glaring at him, trying to smile but there were pink puffs beneath her eyes. "Bastard!" She threw her empty container at him. He caught it and tossed it at the trash basket, missing. "You can pick it up yourself," she said, stalking out.

In a few minutes he followed her. The morning paper was spread out on her desk and she was leaning on one elbow, reading the classified ads. She was smiling now. "Maybe I can find somebody else I can help . . ." she murmured.

Howard laughed and patted her head. The telephone was

ringing and she picked it up. "Mr. Carew's office . . . yes
. . . oh, certainly." She pointed a finger at Howard's chest.
"Mrs. Carew," she said, punching the hold-button. "Good
luck."

Returning to his office, Howard picked up the phone.
"Charlotte? Are you all right?"

"I'm fine," she said. "How are you?"

"Can you hold it just a second?" Putting the receiver
down, he got up and closed the door. "Okay. Where are
you?"

"I still can't tell you, Howard."

"There's something damned unfair about all this," he said.
"If you'd just let me see you—and talk to you, I'm sure we
could straighten it out. I have a lot to tell you."

"Okay. Tell me."

"Not over the phone."

"Then not at all."

"I'm asking you as a favor, as something vitally important
to me . . . Charlotte . . ."

"Tell me what you have to tell me. Then I'll know
whether it's important enough to see you . . ."

"You can take my word for it."

She laughed. "That's very very funny."

"I've broken off with the girl I was—seeing."

"Well you shouldn't have. If you did it for me, you
shouldn't have."

"I did it for her and myself—as well as for you."

"Noble. Look, Howard, I've begun to realize—you haven't
had just *one* affair, you've had about a thousand."

"That's more or less true. That's one of the things I was
going to tell you—how in the hell did you know?"

"Lots of ways. I didn't have any private detective on you,
if that's what you're thinking."

"I know you wouldn't do that sort of thing. What ways?"

"I've been doing a lot of thinking. It's all adding up now."

"For example?"

"The way you've been acting for years. Your idea of an evening at home was to lie in the den and watch a game on television—doing sit-ups to strengthen your stomach muscles. Pounding on your stomach with both fists. I know you weren't strengthening your stomach muscles for *me*. That's just a small thing, of course. There were a lot of small things, and for a long time I thought nothing about them . . ." With a heavy sigh, she broke off.

"Okay, so—" Howard began.

She interrupted him. "One evening about a month ago I called, hoping to catch you before you'd gone. The switchboard was closed and the line was hooked up to Mr. Lorimer's office. He was still there and he answered it himself. He offered to take the elevator all the way down to your office to see if you were still there—a very nice man. We talked for a few minutes—and he said nothing whatever about having dinner with you. So the next morning you told me some story about what a bastard he was with waiters."

Howard found it difficult to reply.

"After that, I found it hard to believe anything you told me—anything you'd *ever* told me."

Howard let a few seconds pass and then in an aggrieved tone he said, "You mean . . . you've been holding this back from me . . . for a whole month . . . without telling me? That was sort of a lousy trick, wasn't it? That doesn't sound like you, Charlotte."

"No, I guess not," she said acidly. "I guess I owe you an apology. Hah!"

"Okay, okay." Howard paused, recognizing the inanity of his position. "Of course you don't. You're beyond reproach. I'm the bastard. That's one of the things I wanted to tell you."

"It's something I've already realized for myself, old friend."

"Damn it!"

"I'm sorry, that's the way I think of you—as my old friend."

For perhaps twenty seconds neither spoke. Then he said, "Charlotte, *please*. Let me see you. Let me tell you what I have to say and then—if that's the end, then okay, I'll accept it, I'll have no choice, I know damned well I don't have a leg to stand on, but please let me see you. Okay?"

There was another long silence. Finally she sighed and said, "Okay. But I should warn you—in all truth and honesty—it won't do you any good. Sorry, Howard . . ."

✳ eighteen

She had agreed to meet him at a restaurant they had often patronized in the past, one only a few miles from the house, which meant, he felt sure, that she had been in Connecticut when she called.

Arriving early, he waited for her on the parking lot and might not have known her if he hadn't known her car. She was wearing a dress he didn't recognize—something pleated and Grecian and pale blue, with a piece of clean white rope at the waist. Her hair was not only longer, it also seemed thicker, and she had done things with it.

"Hi." As she got out of the car, he tried to take her in his arms but she held him off. "Please don't, Howard—my God!" She was staring at him. "It *is* Howard, isn't it?"

"Yes. Who else?"

Her mouth moved. He could tell she was trying to restrain a smile. "I see you got your hair cut, Howard," she said.

"How do you like it?"

"Turn around—what is it? A disguise?"

"Tell me frankly. How does it look?"

"Frankly, it looks horrible. Your hair was always your best feature."

"I decided I wanted to look like myself. No more. No less."

"Well, it's certainly not more," she said. "Maybe quite a bit less." She seemed highly pleased with herself. "Where is your hairpiece?"

"Thrown away." Grimly he took her arm and steered her across the parking lot to the canopied entrance.

The restaurant she had chosen was a place venerating Colonial atmosphere and Connecticut rusticity. It also featured a great many loud white ducks which sported about a waterfall and swam in the pool at its foot. The ducks were offered as an attraction to the drinkers and diners, who were invited to feed them with bread and rolls.

They were led by the hostess to a dining room two levels down, which placed it just below the top of the waterfall. On a still lower level there was a dining room which overlooked the pool.

The evening was warm, the windows were open, and the steady pouring sound of the waterfall was broken now and then with noisy quacking.

Howard looked at his wife across the table, struck by her hair. It looked, he thought, like a hair-do from another century, with tendrils and loops and pieces folded over. It reminded him of a movie he had seen long ago about a blonde courtesan in the court of Louis XIV.

"I like your hair," he said. "Even though you don't like mine. It looks very nice."

"Thank you," Charlotte said.

"Something's different. What is it?"

"It's a hairpiece," she said.

"Oh."

Her eyes showed amusement. "Not funny?"

"I suppose it is." Howard gave her a sad smile. "I feel much too serious about all this to find anything funny. Frankly."

"Frankly?"

"Yes."

A waiter in a red jacket lit their candle and then stood at Howard's elbow.

"I'm not having anything to drink," Howard said. "And I wish you wouldn't. What I have to say is serious." He looked up at the waiter. "Nothing to drink, thanks."

"I hardly know you," Charlotte said. "No hair. No martini."

The waiter returned with menus. Charlotte opened hers and immediately closed it. Howard ignored his. "I'm coming right to the point," he said. "I feel I've made a mess of my life, and I've made a mess of yours."

"I agree," Charlotte said.

"And I'm sincerely and deeply sorry. The least I could have done was let you know what you were married to, instead of posing as something else."

"I'm having the Surf and Turf," she said.

Howard frowned. Her attitude was throwing him off. The waiter was hovering and Howard, as he studied the menu, glanced up to see her eyes filled with amusement. She was looking at his hair. He grimaced. "You say you're having the Surf and Turf . . ."

"Yes," Charlotte said. "The Surf and Turf."

Howard looked hard at the menu, trying to concentrate. "I can't make up my mind." He raised his eyes to the waiter. "My wife is having the Surf and Turf . . ."

"Yes sir . . . and for you?"

"Hell . . ." Howard shook his head with disgust. "Okay. Two Surfs and Turfs." He closed the menu and looked toward the window. The ducks had set up a sudden clamor, perhaps because someone had tossed a piece of bread into the pool. "Okay," he said, "now I'll go on." He lit a cigarette. "As I say, I'm deeply sorry, I really am. I've been a bastard."

Charlotte's eyes were lowered. Looking at her pat of butter, she was smiling faintly.

"Listen," he said, "if all you're going to do is sit there and laugh at my haircut . . . when I'm trying to tell you something in total sincerity and honesty . . ."

"I'm not laughing at your haircut, Howard," she said, and abruptly burst out laughing.

"What's so damned funny?"

She shook her head. "I don't know. Your fervor, I guess. Your total earnestness. You, of all people."

"This is an occasion that calls for a little fervor and a little earnestness, wouldn't you say?"

"Okay, I'm sorry. Maybe if I just don't look at you . . ." With the blade of her knife she began playing with her butter.

"Charlotte . . . no kidding, in all honesty . . . I think you're being bitchy about this. You're not according it any dignity, none at all. This happens to mean a great deal to me."

"I'm sorry, Howard." Still her eyes were shining. "I don't think it's exactly my fault if you happen to pick this very night to show up with a new hairdo. I'm sorry, I just can't get used to it, that's all. I'll keep trying."

Howard let his forehead fall into his palm, rubbing his eyebrows, sighing heavily. Raising his head, he caught sight of their waiter and beckoned him over. "I've changed my mind," he said. "I'll have a martini."

195

The outside lights had come on. The waterfall and pool were brightly lit with floodlights and the effect was theatrical.

While he waited for the martini he looked out at the waterfall, saying nothing. Charlotte seemed perfectly content to remain silent, content to wait.

When the martini arrived, he took a gulp and set it down. "Okay," he said, "I envision something entirely new for us. Now that the abscess is rooted out, now that you know what I am, now that we can be frank with each other, there's no reason why we can't have a much better life than we've ever had before. I'm perfectly sincere about everything I'm saying."

"Yes," she said. "I think you probably are."

"Would you like a sip?" He held the glass out to her.

"No thanks."

Howard smiled. "That dress looks good with your neck," he said. "You've always had a nice neck."

"Thank you."

He studied her face. She was looking down again at her butter, smoothing it with her knife blade, smoothing it and messing it up and smoothing it again. "I don't think I'm getting through to you," he said. "Look—here I am, sitting here before you, totally contrite, totally ready to abase myself. I'm willing to accept the entire blame. I could try to excuse myself. I could recite to you the reasons why I think I did—what I did. But I don't think it would be very dignified. It would sound like self-pity."

"I'd rather you wouldn't go into that part of it," she said.

"I don't plan to." With a feeling of frustration, Howard looked about the room. The place had gotten crowded. The ducks were noisier, the people were louder, the roar of the waterfall more pronounced. He sat there sipping the martini and smoking, saying nothing.

Presently Charlotte said: "Here come the Surf and Turfs—yum!"

Howard turned to her with a pained expression. "*Yum?*"

"Yes. Yum."

"What are you so damned happy about? Are you *glad* about all this?"

"About all what?" She raised her eyebrows. "That we're breaking up our marriage?"

"Who says we're breaking up our marriage?"

"I do."

"Well if we are—are you *glad* about it?"

"Yes—and no. There's something awfully clean about it though. And I'm painting again. That pleases me. For a whole month I couldn't paint a stroke, and it really upset me. I realized what a big part of my life painting really was—and how important it was to your design for living, old friend. While I was painting I was occupied."

Howard remained silent while the waiter set their dinner before them. "Where are you doing all this painting?" he asked as the waiter left.

"Where? I have a wonderful little apartment in the West Village—with a skylight. It's just perfect."

"What are you paying for it?"

"You mean what are *you* paying for it. Or you soon will be. Do you think for a minute I won't be able to get marvelous alimony?"

Howard studied her face as she ate her lobster, trying to decide whether she was putting on an act. Reluctantly he decided that she wasn't. "There's something I have to get through my thick head," he said.

"What?"

"I've got to realize that you're genuinely happy about all this, aren't you?"

She put down her fork and finished chewing. "When a

person decides she's been wasting her life on somebody and then finally reaches a decision to stop wasting it, there's a certain happiness, yes. I can say one thing. I've never felt so free, never felt such a sense of release. Yes, I'm happy. I feel young. I feel clean. I feel very Bohemian—and paint-stained. Last night—"

"What happened last night?"

She held up her hand, she was chewing again. "Last night . . . just for fun, I started a portrait of you—you know, from memory. I was curious to see you tonight. I wanted to see if I had the hairline right. But now . . ." Smiling, she shook her head.

Howard raised a hand to the wedge of naked skin.

"You're not eating your Surf and Turf," she said.

He had stopped eating and started smoking.

"I'll have to cross it out and start a new one," she said.

Howard was looking over his shoulder at the gleaming vertical sheet of water, hypnotized by the endless flow. "A new what?" he asked.

"A new portrait of Howard Carew."

"I never thought you'd take such a bitchy attitude," he said.

She reached across the table. "Let me have a cigarette, will you, Howard?" She took one and he lit it for her. "I'm not a vindictive person," she said. "I don't want revenge. I just want—a better life. How do you suppose it made me feel to know that my husband felt trapped? How do you suppose that would make a woman feel?"

"I never felt trapped."

"You must have. One night I heard you talking in your sleep—something about slave ships and manacled wrists. It was perfectly obvious that you felt you were a prisoner in your own home."

Howard was still looking at the waterfall. He didn't smile. "Excuse me a minute," he said.

"Where are you going?"

"To the men's room," he said. "So-called."

Moodily he threaded his way through the maze of tables and then with heavy step descended a flight of stairs. Out of deference to the Colonial atmosphere, the mirror in the men's room was an antique, with old, rippling glass that gave back a distorted image. With his new haircut he looked grotesque, like an aging clown. For a few seconds he stared at himself in horror. His face withered. With a groan, he turned away.

As he re-entered the dining room, he spotted their waiter and asked him for the check. "Dessert? Coffee? After-dinner drink?"

"No thanks," Howard said. He was looking at Charlotte. Her face was in profile and there was something about her new hair that gave a wonderfully smooth serenity to her brow, softening her face and giving it a patrician quality that overwhelmed him.

"Come back home," he said, sitting down again.

"No. I want a divorce, Howard. And if you have any respect for me you won't make it hard."

"With no kids it should be easy," he said.

Charlotte was lacing and unlacing her fingers. "Don't, Howard."

"I'm not doing anything," he protested. "I'm not doing a damned thing."

"Just don't, that's all."

Howard looked away. Poised at the very top of the waterfall, lit by the floodlights, a large white duck was flapping its wings, quacking raucously.

"Just tell me one thing," he said. "If I hadn't gone under the dining room table that night—and told you—?"

"I don't really know—but I'm glad you told me."

"You say you started getting suspicious the morning I told you I'd had dinner with Lorimer, when you knew I hadn't.

What were you planning to do? For a whole month you
didn't do a damn thing."

Charlotte reached for another cigarette. "I was thinking.
I knew I had to do something but I wasn't sure what. I was
trying to decide, and then I became very curious about the
change that came over you. When you started all that stuff
about truth and honesty, I thought it was just a silly game
you were playing—and then I saw that you were serious
about it. Actually that may have been the key."

"Key? What key?" Howard was still watching the duck
cavort at the top of the waterfall.

"It helped me make my decision. You see, for years and
years you've been so weak and vulnerable, so incredibly self-
absorbed—"

"Thanks."

"I felt responsible for you. Even after I caught you in that
lie I felt it would be cruel to throw you out of the nest, even
though you might damn well deserve it. And then you started
all that truth business and I realized I didn't need to feel responsible for you anymore. I saw you getting stronger. The
night you told off your brother Fred, that was the clincher.
I knew then that I'd be able to leave you if I wanted to, and
then you made it easier by going under the dining room table
and confessing."

Howard nodded. Although he was still looking toward the
waterfall he could see Charlotte playing with her butter again,
smoothing it with the knife blade, rounding its contours. "In
other words, what you're saying . . ." He paused. ". . . is
that if I hadn't started all that truth and honesty stuff . . ."

"I might have gone on for the rest of my life, taking my
half-measure, doing my painting, going to parties and talking
about gypsy moths. . . . So I'm very grateful to you."

She reached for his empty martini glass and held it aloft.
"To truth and honesty . . . Okay, Howard?"

"I say the hell with it," Howard muttered. He turned to the waterfall again. Eyes on the noisy duck, he stood up at the table and flapped his forearms, aware that he was being stared at from the surrounding tables. "Quack, quack, quack!" he called. "Ah! shuddup!"

The waiter was handing him the check, looking at him with curiosity.

"You'll be putting the house up for sale, won't you, Howard?"

"Why not?" He handed the waiter a twenty and waved away the change. "Everything else. Why not the house? Let's get the hell out of here."

He followed her from the room. At the foot of the first flight of stairs, he put his hand under her arm and said, "Nothing left to lose now except my job . . .

". . . and by God, I think I'll quit that," he said as they reached the landing.

"You should have done it years ago," Charlotte said.

"I agree."

As they approached the foyer, he grabbed a handful of free mints and handed her a few. "Come on back to the house," he said. "We'll talk about old times."

She smiled. "No. I'm going home to New York. This is it."

They passed under the canopy and headed across the road toward the parking lot. "I don't need you," he said. "I don't need a damned thing. I'll go climb a mountain. I'll row a boat across the Atlantic Ocean. People do, you know. I'll live off the money I get from the house. You'll get half of it."

"Yes, you've always been very honest about money . . ."

"I always gave you nice Christmas presents . . ."

"Yes, you have a very good heart, Howard." She stopped short and turned. "Something just came over me!" On her face there was an expression of astonishment.

"What is it, for God's sake?"

She opened the door and got in. For a few seconds she just sat there, with a faraway look. "There's no pressure on me to *love* you any more."

"So?"

"It makes it so much easier for me—to like you. I mean, assuming I decide you're likable." She started the motor. "Do you see what I mean?"

Howard reached in and patted her head. "What do we do? Kiss goodbye, or shake hands, or what?"

Charlotte took his hand, raised it to her lips, returned it to him over the windowsill and drove off.

Howard got into his car and followed. He drove with the windows open, letting the breeze flow past his temples. Howard Carew, man of truth, he thought bitterly. He had started his truth program on a whim, and then before he knew it the layers of scotch tape had peeled away. He had come unstuck. I've tried lying and I've tried truth, he thought, and believe me lying is better. He tried to smile at the irony and then asked himself why—why he took flight in laughter, why for so many years he had made mountains out of escapades, why he had filled his life with noise to drown out the silence. Tough questions, but he should look now for the answers. What he found was almost sure to be bleak. It took strength to confront bleakness. Strength and—honesty. But he felt he could do it now.

Half a mile up the road he saw Charlotte's car pulled off to the shoulder. He slowed down as he passed her and was about to stop when, in the rearview mirror, he saw her pull out and follow him.

A few minutes later, as he drew up at a Stop sign, she pulled abreast and called through the open window. "Do you plan to keep your hair like that?"

"I may shave it to the bone," he said.

"Maybe I could start a new portrait of you."

"From memory?"

"Maybe. I don't know. Maybe I'll let you come visit me in my apartment some day."

"I may do that," he said.

"You may find something illicit about it. You may decide it's so sinful that you *enjoy* it."

She cut in front of him and sped off down the road. He sat there, watching her taillights disappear and then drove slowly home, wondering with a lump in his throat if she would be there when he arrived, half-convinced that she would be; but when he got there the parking lot was empty and the house was dark.